PRAISE FOR:

DEIRDRE DANKLIN'S *CATASTROPHE* is hypnotic in its stream of consciousness—haunting, elegant, dark—we swim in and out of reality amid quiet tragedies, seemingly silent, as they take us deep into a mind whose perceptions of the world are like a ghostly fairy tale. Dizzying and magical and painted with poetic prose—dreamy and nightmarish, where the constant struggle with nature and the nature of our memories and experiences intersect with the possibility of hope for a future after sequences of disasters question our existence and humanity, however mysterious. A stunning homage to those we encounter in our lives, nostalgic for our loves, losses, and friendships—Danklin's novella is a reckoning of words, storytelling at its finest."

—SHOME DASGUPTA, AUTHOR OF *SPECTACLE*

"*CATASTROPHE* BY DEIRDRE DANKLIN begins and ends with rain bookends but is about so much more than figurative or natural disasters. In her debut novella, she creates a perfect storm of words, settings, and characters. Danklin skillfully plays with sensory details and poetic prose, emotions and colors splashed throughout: slashes of red, tasting rainbows, baby tongues, blood, rusty desert sand. The award-winning novella is an expert study in contrasts exploring childhood and adulthood, hope and fear, relationship and breakdown, rain and desert. With a deft and often-surprising exploration of classic man v. archetypes, Danklin fills the novella space with her own memorable voice."

—AMY BARNES, AUTHOR OF *MOTHER FIGURES*

"SET IN THE WAKE OF A NEVER-DEFINED catastrophe, Deirdre Danklin's brilliant, gorgeous novella is about living in the tricky aftermath. Part elegy, part fugue, the narration shuttles between two childhood friends who haven't seen each other for years, but who still reach towards each other in their minds. *CATASTROPHE* is a luminous, incisive, profoundly magical book."

—KIM MAGOWAN, AUTHOR OF *HOW FAR I'VE COME*

CATASTROPHE

a novella

Deirdre Danklin

The University Press of SHSU
Huntsville · Texas

Printed in the United States of America
Published by TRP: The University Press of SHSU
Huntsville, Texas 77341
Library of Congress Cataloging-in-Publication Data
Names: Danklin, Deirdre, author.
Title: Catastrophe : a novella / Deirdre Danklin.
Description: Huntsville, Texas : Texas Review Press, [2022]
Identifiers: LCCN 2021045684 (print)
LCCN 2021045685 (ebook)
ISBN 9781680032734 (paperback)
ISBN 9781680032741 (ebook)
Subjects: LCSH: Female friendship—Fiction.
LCGFT: Fantasy fiction. | Novellas.
Classification: LCC PS3604.A5373 C38 2022 (print)
LCC PS3604.A5373 (ebook) | DDC 813/.6—dc23
LC record available at https://lccn.loc.gov/2021045684
LC ebook record available at https://lccn.loc.gov/2021045685
Cover photo details courtesy of dewang_gupta@unsplash
Cover & book design: PJ Carlisle

WINNER OF THE 2021 CLAY REYNOLDS NOVELLA PRIZE

Deirdre Danklin, *Catastrophe*
Selected by Leslie Jill Patterson

*Established in 2001, The Clay Reynolds Novella Prize
highlights one book a year that excels
in the novella format.*

PREVIOUS WINNERS INCLUDE:

Cecilia Pinto, *Imagine the Dog*
Selected by Hannah Pittard

Dylan Fisher, *The Loneliest Band in France*
Selected by Rita Bullwinkel

Patrick Stockwell, *The Light Here Changes Everything*
Selected by Clay Reynolds

The complete list of winners can be found on our website:
texasreviewpress.org

For Hendrik and for my mother

CONTENTS

ONE

I DREAMED OF RAIN LAST NIGHT. I KNOW YOU don't like to listen to people's dreams—no one does. They never make sense—the houses that are like the houses we grew up in, but not quite. The people who are like our parents but with different faces. Anyway, humor me for a minute like you used to. We were in our old backyards playing with sticks. Big sticks like swords, gnarled, covered in spongy blue-green lichen. We were fighting to the death. Inside the house my mother curled up on her bed, a damp washcloth on her head, while my father read a big book about war in the living room. Next door, your sister snuck down a drainpipe, a boy she shouldn't be seeing idling a block away. You were better at fighting than I was. Ruthless, sneaky, you poked me in the stomach with the pointed end of your stick. I was about to surrender, and that's when it started to rain.

Big fat drops of clear water like crystal, splashing rainbows everywhere. We laughed and opened our mouths to the sky. Tasted roygbiv. Little us. Us when we were ten or eleven and you still wore your hair in milkmaid braids. I remember the dewy purple flowers that grew on the edge of our meager woods. I remember how wild we thought we were—like foxes. My father at the back door, his book of war in his hand, yelling come inside! And you, laughing, shaking those braids, saying never, saying no. The two of us put our sticks down and spun in dizzy circles under the colorful rain. Remember when we were schoolgirls? Remember the schoolgirl outfits? You smiled at me, and that's when I woke up. I stared at the metal ceiling of my trailer and tasted rainwater on my tongue. I guess I was thinking of you because of the news—fires in the cities, deaths are reported slowly to the desert. I wonder if it rains where you are. I wonder where you're going to go.

All of our suitcases are packed in the blue morning. The baby is sleeping. My husband is sleeping. I watch the rise and fall of their chests and count the seconds of their breaths. I haven't slept well in months. I pad to the kitchen, turn on the light, turn off the light. Stand still with my feet cool on the tile. I think of you, the first person who ever loved me who didn't have to. I think of your face in the dark. I wonder if you're running away too. We are. Running. My uncle has a cabin—had a cabin—my uncle is dead. I am going and my husband is going and the baby is going. She is an angel of life. Carrying her feels like I'm carrying my organs in a wriggling pile in my arms. She is going, so I go. THE CATSTROPHE is here. That's why we flee. Fires, rats, garbage, death. We can't stay anymore. THE CATSTROPHE is wherever you are too. Disease, murder, overdose, rot. I think I should have written you postcards. Even once I stopped traveling and grew roots

3

from my toes, I should have sent you one postcard per week. I could have bought them online. A picture of Big Ben. A picture of the Taj Mahal. A picture of Niagara Falls. I should have written: how are you? Are you alive? It wouldn't have mattered if you wrote me back or not. That's not the point. The point is, the tile is cool under my feet, and I am afraid. In my quiet house, surrounded by the breath of those I love, I worry. I'm worried about the cat. She's coming too. We're going to hide in my dead uncle's cabin and wait out THE CATASTROPHE. My mother is coming, my sister and her husband and their sons are coming. My family thinks we can wait it out. At least two dogs are coming along with the cat. It's like a sitcom, but we could all die. I can hear the noise in my head before the noise is real. In the blue morning, I stand on the cool floor in silence and I wonder, are you out there somewhere?

I AM IN THE DESERT. THE DESERT IS RED AT dawn. The sand is red and coarse and my heart still loves you, sort of, a lot. There is a lizard's footprint, there is a spider's broken web, there is a two-inch cactus spine. You know me; I am not in the desert because of their catastrophe. I am not in isolation because it is recommended. I am in the desert because I love the indigo sky. I tilted my face up to its great expanse and the sky took me in. I am in the desert because I couldn't make it in a city, in a suburb, in a planned community. Even the places that proclaimed to be weird— *Keep It Weird!*—too much order, not enough counter-culture, not enough wild howling laughter. The billboards didn't sell my kind of weird. My trailer is chrome and it shines. The starlight ricochets off of it. I bet you can't see stars where you're going. I bet when you go to the mountains with your husband and cat and baby and mother and sister and nephews, you will still not see the stars. Did you ever learn to sit in

5

silence? Do you still hate the pauses in conversations? Do you still rush to fill things with your hands? Don't send me a postcard. Don't follow through on the things you think I deserve. Are you still good at fighting? You never heard me, even when I screamed. The sand outside my trailer is red like dried blood, scorpions scuttling, their bulbous tails raised, poisonous. And a many-legged, many-eyed church singing for rain into the desert darkness. Go ahead, you run for the trees. I'll stay here. We'll see who makes it out of this. I hope that it's you.

The car is so quiet I can hear the wheels turn. Even the baby, wide-eyes, pink mouth, is sleeping. My husband looks tired. Circles under his eyes. Frown. Once, we didn't sleep you and I. The dawn broke on our faces, but we never looked tired. Was it just being young? There is a lot of traffic driving out of the city. Scattering to the trees. Remember the woods behind the school—that ring of mossy stones you found? Trying to cut our palms with safety scissors? Once we're past the highway, we're past the other people. Everyone is slouching, trying to hide in their cars. The dawns here are gray now, not pink. A knot blooms at the center of my stomach. It pulls tighter and tighter. Kissing my husband tastes like blood. Loving something is living with death. Around us, trees rise up. They pity us, I imagine. We are fleeting and fragile. Trees would tell us things, if they could, about roots. And now I think we might die out here in this green space. That seems better, better than dying in a rootless apartment owned by someone else. Everything I own was once owned by someone else: my car, my clothes, my husband's love. Not the baby, though. She's brand new, uncreased. I am creasing her. I am the first owner of her morning smiles. Maybe I shouldn't think of my baby that way. If you were here, I'd tell you to do her astrological chart. Write her a story. Read tea leaves,

7

spread tarot cards or entrails. And I know you'd do it. Like the rabbit in that mossy ring of stones. I chickened out, my wrist too weak, my hands shaking. And you said I was better at fighting because I didn't hesitate. We never found out what the rabbit's insides would have told us. Maybe the rabbit would have told me about this silent car ride, the hush of the wheels, the pine trees growing taller, and the circles underneath my husband's eyes.

I STILL HEAR YOU, YOUR THOUGHTS, everything, this whole time we've been apart. Years of your thoughts. Years of your love for other people, clear and sharp as a silver bell. Ringing in my head. Running for the woods, a circle of mossy stones. But here, the girls who tumble across the desert beg to have their cards read. This morning, a freckled girl in braids but too old for it, chewing her bottom lip, wondering if her man is a ticket out, to somewhere where it rains. He's not. He's not. They never are. You're your own ticket, I tell her, Gangly, but she doesn't want to hear it. She only wants to hear that one day she'll wake up and it'll all be different. Better. It's the kind of thing the church tells her to expect—instant miracles. She doesn't want to hear about the gentle slide, the gradations on a colorwheel until you wake up and everything is dust red when once it was ocean blue. I used to live by the ocean, did I tell you that? I forget sometimes, you can't hear. The safety scissors, your blood in the cut on the palm of my hand. That's when you started sounding clear as a silver bell. I didn't realize a girlhood pledge would mean forever. What's forever when you're fourteen? I used to live by the ocean and read girls' tea leaves. The ocean girls didn't want to leave their lives as much as these desert girls do. They wanted, instead, to know if they were ever going to have an experience that would change them, rock them, shake them so hard their bones would never sit right again.

Volcano moments. Of course, we all have those days, those years. They kill us sometimes. I remember the rabbit's beating heart. Rabbits will die rather than be devoured. I went back after you failed and spread its guts out on a mossy rock. I ran my fingers through the blood to read the fuzzy message. Be afraid, the rabbit told me, but maybe that's what all rabbits think looking into the glint of a girl's knife-point.

The cabin is made out of logs. It's very burnable. But far enough from the treeline to be safe from the fires, my husband says. The windows soar. Around us is wilderness. Beyond that, the shadows between trees. At the bottom of the mountain spreads a clear lake. My husband read about the lake on the internet. It is man-made; it drowned a town. Rich people have vacation houses there. I suppose my uncle was rich when he was alive, but he lived alone. Now we're here, the messiness of us: the unpacking, the unfolding, the upstairs, the downstairs, the honey where's the . . . of it all. My mother, my father, my sister, the kids, the dogs, one cat yowling, afraid, in her travel carrier. There is no quiet here, even though the cabin sits on top of a hill inside a ring of trees. It's a good spot for magic, is what I mean, if there could just be quiet. The baby is quiet—she looks at me with her glacier-clear eyes as if I know the answer. As if we two live in a bubble of silence, protected. The sunscreen is in my purse. The bug spray rolling loose on the floor of the passenger side of the car. Baby in a travel crib. We take the bedroom downstairs. My husband likes our chances in case the cabin goes up in flames. My sister, still bossing me like we're children, still sneaking out of the house. Her boys, running wild, crayons in hand, saying they want to get lost in the woods, saying they want to start over with sasquatch. My father laughing, he doesn't believe in THE CATASTROPHE, saying sasquatch was a hippie, unloading his new silicone bong, quarantined in the garage. Smoke to hover over the adults' heads. The baby and I sit on our bed. I am immovable. She is still. My husband carries in the suitcases, the cat. I let her out of her crate and she hides. I start unfolding all of our clothes. I lay them out around me as, in the hall, the boys shout that they want a sailboat for the clear lake, that they want to touch the tip of the drowned church steeple. Remember the catholic services we sat through in school? The red of the wine we were allowed to drink even when we were eleven because it wasn't wine anymore it was blood. Remember how, when we were eleven, we took a boat out onto a lake, a different lake, a natural lake, and watched fish open and close their mouths? When we were seventeen and at a party by that lake and you pushed a guy into the water. A guy you said was creepy but who everyone else liked. My husband comes into the bedroom and sees me and the baby sitting on the bed in a circle of unfolded clothes. So many of her clothes are pink. Like blood mixed with water. What are you doing?–my husband wants to know. I'm checking that everything's here, I tell him. We have to share one dresser. At home I have a whole closet of clothes I haven't worn in months. Inside, it's all cotton and stretch and baby stains. The baby lifts her eyes up to her father and smiles. We love him, his beautiful girls. I think about the ring of trees surrounding this cabin. I wonder if the distance and the quiet and the ghost of my uncle's money can keep us all safe.

TOO MANY PEOPLE IN YOUR CABIN; IT'S JUST
me in my trailer. When I lived by the ocean there were four
other girls, heads-shaved, tattooed, tasting of salt. One slept in
my bed. She drew on my arms with colored markers. She said
she saw us in the constellations, holding hands. But, there was
a chilly distance there. After you, I never got out my safety

13

scissors again. Not so safe. I left because I couldn't stand the waves. In and out. In and out. The girl's faces changed. New roommates, new lovers, new beds, new drawings. Nothing was constant, everything moved. I wanted to find a burrow where I could sit still. Cry less. By the ocean, sand in my toes, I drank an entire bottle of wine on my own and called for a creature to rise up from the sea. Nothing ever came for me, even though I was sure something would. Claim me, monsters! Once, a new roommate brought a baby. Like your baby. Big eyes, but not quiet. The baby screamed and screamed like it knew something we didn't. Or, like it knew the same things we did, but it hadn't gotten used to them yet. I moved to the desert after the girl with the markers left me. I chopped off my hair. I put everything I owned in one suitcase. I still don't own much. Here in this place, girls still wash up, blown in on the wind. Here, I shuffle my cards and tell them their stories, but I stay the same, like you now, immovable. Today, the gangly girl in braids is back. She's mad at me. Mad at the future. She wants a re-do. So, I shuffle her cards again. I ask her what she'd like me to say. Her eyes light up, then, a spark. She hadn't realized that she could just ask for what she wanted. What do you want? And she says she wants to matter. A young person's response. Are we still young? I feel ancient, like a rock formation hewn from a mountain by wind. I guess older people would roll their eyes at that. My elbows aren't so bendy anymore. I remember the catholic masses, do you remember the cartwheels? You were too afraid to launch yourself upside down. I remember the wine. I still drink it alone, but no creature has ever walked out of the desert for me, either. No angel with wisdom, terrible, covered in eyeballs, has ever claimed me a prophet. I tell the gangly girl that it's not enough to want to matter, she has to be more specific. She says she wants to feel like her life means something, do I know what she means? She wants to feel like she has a purpose. I reach all of my spiritual feeling out towards her plain little nose, then, but there's nothing there. No flame. Not even a small one like you had at first, when I took out my safety scissors that day. I'd never be able to hear this girl in my head. Or, maybe I could train her. Is it loneliness that makes me think of it? What do you think will make you matter to people?—I ask her. She says, knowledge, which isn't a bad answer. I read her cards for her, then, and I lie. I tell her she'll learn something important very soon, but who knows? Who can tell when the lessons will come? My lessons all came early, fell like stones on my young body. I never liked that guy, he had eyes like a wolf, I was right to push him in the lake. It's not distance that keeps people safe. Nor quiet, nor money. People can climb up your mountain. It's fear. There's a small town nearby, a whole congregation buried in red sand, but the gangly girl is the first visitor I've had in weeks. Why? Because I make people fear.

At breakfast, everyone emerges from their rooms, rubbing their eyes. I made pancakes. My baby smiles at her father and at her grandmother but frowns at her cousins. The boys look like it's an adventure—pancakes, the woods! The adults carry tension in their shoulders, scanning the trees. My mother institutes a new rule at the wide wooden table: no phones or laptops before noon. She doesn't want to know what's going on in the world at the bottom of the mountain. How did my uncle make the money to buy this house? Investments, my father said. Investments in what? But my father didn't answer. A memory flashes in my mind. It can't be a real memory, though it feels real. You and me in my parents' house. A crunching sound. We peer around the corner into the kitchen and there is my mother, fully dressed, chewing on her pearl necklace. The pearls become dust in her mouth. They crunch like crackers. I know this memory isn't real because right now my mother is wearing her pearl necklace at the table, telling my sister that the news is toxic, but I swear it happened. I can hear the pearls crunching. My husband puts his hand on my lower back, asks if I'm okay. I'm tired, I say, which is my excuse for everything. Has been since the baby came, even though she's docile and good. My sister and mother have formed a truce. My sister can read the news on her phone in the bathroom with the door locked. But she can't tell anyone what's going on until after lunch. I don't want to know, but I'll be able to tell how bad things are by my sister's facial expressions. She never could keep a secret. Sneaking back into our childhood home, she made a racket loud enough for the whole neighborhood to hear. Investments in what?–I ask my father again, but he shrugs. He's annoyed that I want to know. It's all in my dead uncle's papers somewhere. I can take a look if I care so much.

DOG AND I SIT AND WATCH THE HOT SUNRISE. Living in the desert, I've gotten used to the heat. Have you? We used to sit on the air vents in your parents' kitchen and pretend we were shrinking glaciers. I don't remember your mother eating her pearls, but it sounds like something she would do out of spite. Or fear. If she had a pearl necklace, my mother wouldn't bother chewing, she'd swallow them whole. I have to remind myself to put on clothes today because Megan is coming. Sometimes I live in a long shirt no underwear, me and Dog and the trailer. We smell like animals. Now that the catastrophe is here, people drive up less and less. Although, the other day, I did get a woman, mascara down her cheeks, who wanted to know if hell was real. I told her that I didn't think so. She said that was good because she was going to kill somebody. I didn't ask her who, I don't need that kind of drama in my life. When Megan shows up, she's carrying something cupped in her hands. I can tell, even from a distance, that it's sick. It's a lizard. A pet lizard, she says. Her little brother's pet gecko. Its name is Giles, Giles the gecko. He's dying. Can I save him? I look at Megan's face. She's got a new sunburn on her nose, dead skin peeling away from her freckles. The sun will kill her. I tell Megan to bring Giles the gecko inside. Dog sniffs at her hands but doesn't lunge. He's useless as a guard dog, even though he's big, but he's good at comfort. If the catastrophe hadn't happened I could put a vest

18

on him and trot him around an old folks' home. I put Giles
on the Formica folding table in what, I guess, is my kitchen.
Megan is biting her lip and blinking hard. What's the deal
with the gecko?–I ask. It's her little brother's gecko. Her little
brother who hung himself last year. Okay. I put my hand
over Giles the gecko. It's such a little thing to heal. He's old
for a gecko. Weak. Maybe I should let him die, but I think
of the dead skin on Megan's nose. I let a little pulse of light
into Giles' body. He'll be a very long-lived gecko. There's no
real change in him, lying flat on the table, but Megan can tell
he's better. He blinks his moist eyes at us. I wonder about a
gecko's thoughts. I wonder if geckos think of rain. His toes
are cute. Megan thanks me, wipes her nose. It was nothing,
I want to say, but of course, even this small revival will cost
me. I'll be exhausted the rest of the day. Megan wants to tell
me about her dead brother, but I can see it all in her head.
His feet dangling. His neck broken, his face not the kind of
dead face that people say looks asleep. I put up my hand to
stop her words. I don't need words. We use animals to tell
ourselves things we want to hear. Megan goes to get Giles'
terrarium. It's in the trunk of her car. She was so upset that
she drove over here with Giles in her lap. As if saving the
lizard is the same as lifting her little brother's legs in time,
breathing life back into his purple body. Giles blinks at me
but I'm not sure he's too grateful. Dog approves though, of
my mercy, he always approves because he's simple. Megan
wants me to teach her to read cards today, but I'm tired. The
gecko is walking around with some of me inside it—leaving
a hollow in my chest. I tell her to go and come back some
other time. She asks me what she's supposed to do all day.
She got fired when the one supermarket in town still open

19

closed down a week ago. She lives with her junkie mother in a collapsing ranch house. I tell her to read a book. She laughs. She says she'll be back tomorrow. When she passes Dog on the way back to her car, he lifts his head and wags his tail. She leans over and pets him. Dog is easy to please. The sun rises higher. It's getting hotter.

My sister has organized activities for us on a color-coded whiteboard calendar. She's concerned that we'll get on each other's nerves in the cabin. We will. It's inevitable. But, there are puzzles and crayons and board games and decks of cards ready to go. The boys are color-coded red like a warning. Distraction is meant to keep us from each other's throats. The boys want none of their mother's games. They want the woods, bad. Boys raised in a suburb, trees ringed with fences and concrete, want to lick the sap from wild bark. I can see my sister flinch at the nature-hunger in her boys' eyes. She's afraid of the leafy shadows, stray animals, the rot. Things die in the woods and mushrooms explode from the corpses. I'm afraid too, but also compelled. We should go on a hike, I say, and the boys pick up the word like a chant. A hike! A hike! My sister wants to say no, to say, let's stay inside and play board games, safe. But, she's overruled. So, then it's twenty minutes of: put on your shoes, tie your shoes, put on bug-spray, put sunscreen on your nose. My mother and father stay behind, too old, but the young families go. My husband and I used to hike all the time. I'm good at going uphill, he's good at going down. As soon as we leave the cabin the boys run towards the trees. Be careful!—my sister shouts, is doomed to shout for the rest of her life at the backs of her running boys. The woods are cool and calm. Still a few birds singing, and that makes me relax, birds never sing when predators come. When death comes. I read this somewhere

21

once and I believe it, even though all the crows and pigeons and mourning doves on the phone wires back home never stopped gossiping when THE CATASTROPHE killed our neighbors. My husband wears my baby on his back in a harness and her legs dangle, chubby, and her eyes take in the woods in all seriousness. The boys pick up big sticks, pretend to fight, one whacks the other over the head a little too hard. Hey boys, come on, their mellow father says, so they agree to be on the same team and wield their sticks to protect us. Their father was the first good man my sister ever brought home, and we were all so, so relieved to see the kindness in his eyes. I like walking in the woods. Even when we were children. The roots talk to me, tell me that they've been there for a long time, growing for a long time, and that they'll be there long after I'm gone. My baby looks at me like she can hear them too. Then, a snap. A footstep. Bigfoot!—yells the older boy, but of course not. Of course, it's a mother deer and her baby. The baby is so small, spotted, fragile-looking. We all stop and stare. Breath held. The air here isn't as warm as it is in the city. In the city a man, Chuck, who's addicted to fentanyl, sits in the alley behind my friend's house and screams at the sky. I want to die, Chuck screams. Maybe he is dead. Maybe THE CATASTROPHE got him. It has been a while since I sat on my friend's back porch. The mother deer flicks her ear towards us, every muscle in her body ready to spring away, but she can tell that we're not a threat. She dips her head to chew on something green. Her baby stares at us, black liquid eyes, without any fear. Cool!—the younger boy breathes, and we agree, yes, it's cool to see a wild animal. We don't see animals except squirrels or rats or our dogs or the cat. But this is an animal that exists without us, that does not depend upon us. She and her baby. I wish her well. We walk deeper into the woods, but we're on a trail that's a loop. A trail that was paved for the rich people whose dark homes loom near my uncle's. We don't see anyone else. Besides the few birds and our footsteps and the boys' shouts, the woods are silent. There is a gate at the bottom of the mountain. There is a code we had to punch in to drive up. The code was in my dead uncle's will. He said we could use it if we ever needed. We were all he had left. The trail leads us back to the cabin in time.

MEGAN COMES FILLED WITH ADMIRATION
because I saved her dead brother's gecko. I want to tell her
that the pulse of life from my hands exacts a price. I spent the
rest of the day yesterday felled by a migraine. Like my mother.
It'd been a long while since I'd given to anything else. That
part of me has grown weaker. But Megan wants it all, right
away. She wants to learn to cure geckos with her hands, and
more. She wants to save the drug addicts and the dying trees.
She wants to bring the water back to her town. And the jobs
and the money. She wants to stand in front of the rockslide
that is this moment, with her hands outstretched, and stop
it from destroying the place and people that she loves. She
can't. I can tell she doesn't have it in her. No magic power.
She's bone dry. Useless. Except to keep me company. So, I
take the cards out. I tell her I'm going to teach her how to
read, but I don't tell her that real reading isn't about cards at
all. I pretend there's a story behind the images and sequences.
That it matters which card I pull. It doesn't. It never has.
All the cards mean the same thing: change, rebirth, death,
rebirth, change. Nothing else. The real reading is in people.
I can read Megan's open face, her defenses down now that
I saved her gecko so easily, she thinks. She spent last night
curled up in her childhood bed, still sexting with the man
who moved away weeks ago. The man who is going to get
with a redheaded waitress in a month or so. He's got a thing
for redheads, his favorite cousin was a redhead, but he tries
not to think about it like that. Megan furrows her brow at

the cards and makes a face to let me know that she's trying hard to understand. I don't tell her, either you're born with it or you're not, because I don't want her to say again, no fair! Of course it's not fair. Nothing is fair. Even when we try to make it so. I miss trees. I'm jealous of your woodland walk. The paved trail is a monstrosity, but still, you have cool wind on top of that mountain, and a few birds, and two deer. Green things still grow from the ground. Green things that might need me, I remind you. That's why I'm out here and not in the city, in the woods, near the ocean. Did I ever tell you about the whale? Let me tell you, like the old days when I used to make you try: testing, testing, testing! Listen up about the whale. Right before I packed everything and left the oceanside. It died. It rotted. The stench soaked the air. Things came from all over to eat it. It writhed with bodies taking bites. I watched from the boardwalk. The girl with the colorful markers drew a whale on my arm and said–That's you. It's like you. And I couldn't wash the wet stink off my shirt for weeks. Out here in the desert nothing reaches its green tendrils toward me, begging for life, a spark, a bite, screaming give me some of your light. Like that boy with the wolf-eyes who I pushed into the lake. I think this one means death, Megan says, pointing to a card, a devil, red and pointy-eared, drawn on its middle. The devil's not death, but I don't tell her that. I say, very good. Death, change, rebirth, death, change, that's all there is. Remember when you asked me if I could fix that scar on your forehead and I kissed it and it disappeared? I've never fixed another scar. I let them all stand witness. Megan smiles at me like she learned something, I let her think that she has.

In the middle of the night, a man walks out of the woods and into the cabin. He's an outsideman—that's my first thought. He looks like he belongs outside. Like Chuck. A scraggly beard sprouts from his face, he looks shocked, electrocuted. The beard is gray, his nose has age spots on it. His limbs are sinewy, ropey, too much labor and sun. He sets off the alarm. It's all scramble, scramble, where's the baby? My brother-in-law hefted an iron skillet over his head. My sister brandished a knife. The outsideman held up his hands, woah, woah, he came in peace. He used to know my uncle, he said. He didn't know that my uncle died. When we told him, he hung his head. Then we all stood there with our weapons (not me, I had the baby) and stared at his sadness. He had nowhere else to go. He had a tent on his back. My uncle used to let him sleep on the lawn. Could he sleep on the lawn? I felt it, the fear and shame, creep over all of us. We looked to my father even though we're grown. He nodded his head, wanting to be good. Wanting to share his weed. Give that old man a hit. The young hippies let him smoke for nothing because once he flipped a car over on the George Washington bridge to protest Vietnam. My mother opens her mouth like she's going to forbid it, she's where all the real family power is, but then she closes it. It takes her a beat to open it again. Do you need a blanket?–my mother asks. I bounce the baby, now awake and fussing, in front of the window. We watch the outsideman set up his tent where the deer walked into the lawn. My husband puts his hand on the small of my back. Kisses our baby. I lean into the warmth of him. The strength. Tall man safe. You think he's okay?—I ask my husband. The outsideman doesn't look like a drug addict. My husband worked with drug addicts in the city. Fentanyl, sways, bends, heroin, yellow eyes, yellow teeth, flashes of violence, oceans of remorse. This guy looks like he could survive even if THE CATASTROPHE wipes people like us off the face of the Earth. My husband yawns. Go, go to bed, I tell him. Everyone else is in bed. The boys stayed in their room, barricaded when they heard the alarm. Ready to fight with tiny fists and thrown sneakers. My baby smiles. She loves her daddy, but she and I are the same body. I bounce her and kiss her head, and the two of us watch the outsideman. Then, the motion-sensor lights go off and it's dark again. Dark like it never is in the city. So dark, I can't see his tent or the ring of trees. All I can see is my own reflection, me and my baby in the glass of the door.

I'M ALONE AT NIGHT. AWAKE BECAUSE I HEARD your alarm in my head. *Wee-ooo wee-ooo.* I try to think of you surrounded by your family. I remember your rebellious sister. Too much pot, sneaking out using drain pipes, getting her bedroom window nailed shut. Now she's a boy-mother—two boys. It makes me laugh to think of it. Now she'll be the one trying to cage, to hem-in, to tame youth's wildness. I imagine you bouncing your baby, in my head, you look too young for it. It strikes me as sad that I'll never *see* your face wrinkle and spot. You're forever seventeen. Except for your voice, your thoughts—those have changed. One thing the desert has that the forest doesn't is stars. Acres and acres of unobscured stars. Naked and spread over the desert, no trees in the way, no buildings, no smoke, hardly any light. Since the catastrophe, my trailer light flickers like a lone flame in the darkness. There used to be a Supermarket and a Super Walmart near the cluster of houses where Megan lives. People in cars, campers and trailers used to squat in the parking lots, running their engines, their headlights, clogging up the night with their homey desperation, but they're gone now too. Just alot of bleached bones in the desert now. Silence. Out here, it's just me and Dog. Sometimes I go out with Dog in the night. He's good. He whimpers by my side when I go out far, farther. It's hard to tell how far when everything is so flat. Then, I lie down and look at the stars. Obscene stars. Have they been overhead this whole time? How old were you when you first saw the milky way? Did it scare you, all the pulsing light?

I'm not scared. I'm not sure I can feel scared anymore. Dog huffs down beside me in the sand. He rests his jowls on my ankles and waits. He thinks there's going to be a coyote or a wolf or a man with a chainsaw and he's going to have to be Brave Dog and save us both. But I know nothing is coming. That's another side effect of the catastrophe, emptiness. Death. All the wild things dying. I wonder how long until Dog and I are the last warm bodies left. It used to be too cold in the desert at night. I'd freeze if I went out to lie on my own. Not anymore. I look up at the stars and imagine myself spinning in space. Imagine how small I am, me and Dog and the little pulse of light that I carry with me, that thing you called power that time by the lake. Magic power. What good is it? Revive dead lizards. Retreat to the desert. Let girls with multicolored markers hurt me. Tiny bites of darkness. I let you leave me and go silent, except for your thoughts in my head. My mother told me before she died that she could move things with her mind. Her head hurt and she lay down and she whispered, I can move things—but my father said it was a side-effect of the pills, those thoughts, that she couldn't change anything, no matter how hard she tried. But now I wonder, maybe she *could* move things, maybe she had a magic power so small, so human, that it could only move little things. A feather, a teabag, maybe a shoe. What good is magic power like that? What good is it just lying in bed with a cool washcloth on your head? The stars above me tell me to be quiet, to sink into the sand, but I keep thinking my thoughts at you, waiting for the sun, wondering if somehow you'll hear. In the distance, for a moment, I think I hear a wolf howl, but it's just the wind.

Now my sister doesn't want the boys to go outside because the outsideman is there. He slept in his tent, his feet poked out. His feet were in sandals, but they were dirty. Maroon with dried blood and dirt. How long did he walk to get to our mountain? Why is the mountain ours? Did I sleep? Did the baby? It's hard to say. I haven't slept well since THE CATASTROPHE started. Not since the baby was born, either. A little miracle. Wide-eyed, looking at me for information. How do you explain THE CATASTROPHE to a baby? I bet you'd be good at it. Like it isn't a big deal. You'd say, people made the wrong choices and here we are. Here we are. Another catastrophe. Don't make it THE CATASTROPHE. My sister can't keep the boys inside. They're little animals and the woods are all around us, beckoning. Is there a town at the foot of the mountain?—my sister asks, we don't know. Did we drive by a Dollar General, a Super Walmart? A McDonald's neon sign blinking its last in the dark? I don't remember driving through anything. I remember the dawn and the trees. My sister wants to know if there are authorities she can call about the man in the tent. Maybe there's a kind local sheriff in the town at the foot of the mountain. A nice warm jail cell. We raise our eyebrows at her. We live in the city, there are no kind authorities. The cops would shoot him, my husband says. If there are still cops. Maybe, once everything got started, they all shot each other. So, we stand in silence at breakfast. Shame. Do you think he has enough to eat?—my mother asks. The boys run out with cereal in a bowl, milk in a bottle, before my sister can stop them. It's an adventure! It's like seeing a bear! Their kind-eyed father goes with them. We all watch while they hand the man a spoon. The boys go zooming into the green lawn. How did my uncle make his money? Then a flash, investments. Investments in what? Green is good for growing kids. I carry my baby in my arms, she presses her chubby hands to the glass door. An image flashes, me in middle school, pressing my hands to the door of your math class, telling you with my mind that it was time to run. How different our childhoods were. There were catastrophes, but they were farther away. When the planes hit the towers my mother said: none of this has anything to do with you. You remember when we left math class and ran into the woods and stretched our arms out as far as they would go? I'm a peregrine falcon, I said. I'm the wind, you said. The outsideman wolfs his cereal and my brother-in-law ushers the boys back inside. What did he say?—my sister asks, her face creased with indignation and worry. She imagines the man with a knife, with a rope, hurting her boys. It takes one night for her to go from being crazy to being right. He said thank you, my brother-in-law says.

IN THE MORNING, DOG AND I WAKE UP WITH sand in our noses. No critters came by in our sleep. No scorpions, no flies, no spirits with hungry mouths. The oddest thing about the catastrophe is the dying off of all the small things. I'd become so used to their little voices. Hums. Buzzes. Now, not even a car whirring by. No rumbling tires. No horns or alarms. The catastrophe is silence. Silence closing its fist around us. When we were kids I used to listen to see if I could hear ghost voices at night. Don't close your eyes, I told you, but I closed mine, waited in the dark and listened. I listened, but I never heard anything, well, once, maybe. I don't think Megan is coming today. I think she wants to give me space and I appreciate that, but I also want her to move in with me and Dog. I want her to sew us matching nightshirts. I've always just want someone to stay with me. That's not true. Not specific enough. I wanted *you* to stay. Maybe my mother. I remember being the wind in the woods. I remember you being a falcon. Falcons have eyes that can see and see. You didn't see enough, is what I think. That's what I would tell you if you could hear me. You don't see enough. Is your sister the only one who thinks the outsideman is bad news? How did your uncle make his money? Once, when I lived by the ocean, there was a dead and rotting whale—I know told you that. But it lingers in my mind, the image of it, the stench. That's you, the girl with the colorful markers said. Dog and I get up and shake ourselves all over. Nothing but dead sand falls away. I'm grateful not to be bug-bitten—I don't miss the mouths, but I miss the astonishing variety of them. So, silence. Back to silence. I can feel the little pulse of light back under my skin. Recovered from healing the gecko. I should heal something else. I should fix one small thing a day. Remember when I pushed that boy in the lake? The one who raped that girl. The girl they found the next year. The girl we never talked about. The one our mothers warned us not to be. Face on a telephone pole. Lucky to get even that much attention. I think she was the one true ghost voice I ever heard. Her raw anger on the cool surface of the lake. Anger like a mirror. You should have drowned him, the voice said. It used to be that tragedies were shocking and we all could pretend they happened rarely. The boy went to jail, I think. What's going to happen to jails now? Have all the prisoners died, locked in, abandoned? Did they all break out, now that the world is one big silent catastrophe? I should have drowned that wolf-eyed boy. Too late. It's too late now. Dog whines at my feet for food, so I feed him. And that's love. I feed him and I stroke his silky ears while he eats. I ask him dumb questions in the dumb voice people use for dogs. Who's a good boy? Who is? He ignores me. I remember your hands pressed against the glass of my math classroom's door. Your voice in my head. The door to my trailer has a window. Come press your hands against it. You can bring the husband and the baby, just as long as you bring your face, and take me to the woods with you. Tell me you're the peregrine falcon. Tell me I'm the wind.

We spend the afternoon inside, a family huddled together, craning our necks to watch the outsideman. He doesn't do much. He sits in the sun and chews a long blade of grass. My fingers itch watching him. Why doesn't he have a book to read? Music to listen to? Something to stare at? He's staring at the trees. He looks like a monk on a rock. It looks like he tells weary mountain climbers that the answers they're looking for are waiting back at home. My sister is making the boys stay inside. They hate it, but then they decide to play hide and seek. My baby squeals as they whizz through the cabin. Then, I remember, investments. I ask my husband to watch out for the baby. I'm afraid that when I leave the room she ceases to exist. Like she's a part of me that blips in and out depending on whether I'm looking at her or not. I'm almost always looking at her. My uncle's study. Sneaking. Remember when we used to sneak? We broke into the vice principal's office, but then we just felt sad for her. She had a framed picture of her ruddy-colored dog on her desk. Mismatched pens in a mug that said "WORLD'S BEST AUNT!" I'm not the world's best aunt. The boys are laughing, giving the game away by how much noise they're making. I shush them as I walk deeper into the bowels of the cabin. I feel the pull of my baby in my belly like a taut string. I should go back to her. I should make her blip back into existence. Or she should make me blip, either one. I'm not sure. But, I'm curious. I've been curious since my father said I could look if I care. I walk

34

into the office. One of my nephews, the younger one, red hair, curly, shy, shy, shy, is hiding behind a stack of plastic three-ring binders. He wants to laugh so badly, but he's got his fingers stuffed in his mouth to keep himself from giving his hiding spot away. I look at him and put my finger to my lips. He nods, his eyes watery with hilarity. I open the first binder I see. It's acid green. Inside, the paper is covered in numbers. I don't understand it. I open another with a contract in it. A contract for land. This land? Whose mountain was this before it belonged to my uncle? I'm about to flip the page when my other nephew, the older one, blonde and broad-shouldered, so handsome that if we're not careful he'll grow up to be an asshole, bursts in. He can see his brother's flame-bright hair. There you are! Got you!—he shouts and my red-headed nephew pulls his fingers from his mouth. He laughs like letting the air out of a balloon. *Hahahahahahaha.* Remember when I laughed so hard I fell over drunk? That's how I got that scar you kissed away. The boys scamper out and, without them, the office feels sinister. I take the binder with the contract in it and leave. I'll ask my husband. He's the one who knows about businesses. Nonprofits. How not to make a profit. All I know is how to fix a child's sentence. How to break it. Break it again. Paste it back together. I used to think it was important for people to know how to read, write. If we could just communicate better. My baby looks up at me when I re-enter the living room. Her eyes say, I almost stopped existing, Mama. I reach my arms out and scoop her in close to my heart. I drop the binder on the floor. What's that?—my husband asks. Dunno. A contract. He opens it and frowns in concentration. Outside, I can hear the outsideman whistling. This is the name of the town we drove through, my husband says, pointing to a word. I don't care anymore. I bury my nose in my baby's hair. Breathe the sweet newness of her head. Do I care? Do I care what bought us our safety? We should go outside, I say. I don't think that guy is going to hurt us.

HOW LONG IS IT BEFORE MEGAN COMES BACK
again? I don't know. Without other people, time slips by
me like I'm on a boat and time is the water. *Whoosh*. It rolls
right off. But, then she's here. Shy. Stubborn. Freckles. I
want so badly to fix things for her. Maybe if I pulsed a little
light into her mother, maybe if I pulsed a little light into the
congregation. But, no, there are too many of them. The last
of the last people have formed a circle at the center of the
small town. A closed fist of people. Like sand crabs, they're
most active at night. I hear them singing their eerie songs
about the end of the world. Megan is the only one who leaves
their circle now. She's brought me cans of beans as though she
thinks I don't have food. A good sign—the church doesn't
know about my pit of nonperishables. Unperishable. I was
wondering if you could teach me how to heal things?–Megan
asks, her voice a trembling bird. No, I say, too advanced. But
what I mean is, not ever, never. You can't have it if you're
not born with it. Magic is elitist. I remember that time you
fell over drunk and got that scar. I could never get drunk
no matter how hard I tried. I can still hear you saying that
the stars were swinging overhead, swinging in a circle, that it
was amazing to watch, terrifying, and I was envious of how
drunk you were. Megan says, please. She's not usually so
polite. She's been making demands of me since she showed up.
Please. She wants to heal the town and a mother addicted to
drugs. She wants to bring water and green life to this barren
place, unclench the fist at its center. Make the congregation

happy. And I say, that's nice. It's nice to want to help. But, what can you do? What can you do against the indifferent eyes of nature? I remember lying next to you on the grass and whispering to myself, *you're drunk too, you're drunk too.* But all the whispering in the world couldn't make it true. It pisses me off that I'll never once get to use drunkenness as an excuse. To make her feel better, I told Megan I'd teach her more about telling people the future. What good is it if they never listen?—she asks, and I'm thinking there's something specific there. Yes. In purple flashes. Bruises on the arms of a junkie mother. Purple blooming on the dead ankles of her hanging brother. The same purple as the absence of her never-known father. He blew away on the wind and left three people in his dust. Her hatred for him is purple too, like lips starved of oxygen. This might be useful. I say, sometimes they listen. Sometimes, when it's important. She says that there are people in the church, the tightest part of that tightly-clenched fist, who are going to kill themselves at the end of the month if it doesn't rain. This makes me laugh. I sound like Dog. A bark of a laugh. Megan smiles and rubs her arms with her hands, looks at the ground. When was the last time it rained? I tell her to come inside. They don't mean it, I tell her. They're just talking. Make tea. Lean into the silence of it. I remember lying next to your drunk body, in silence, wanting to see the stars spin. I remember when that tall blonde boy came over, also drunk, and he said you were the most beautiful thing he'd ever seen. You laughed at him, but that red crept up your neck. So clear, unblurred. I never could get drunk. Megan and I drink the tea even though it's one hundred degrees out, but I tell her it's the leaves that are important. The leaves that have touched a person's mouth. Those leaves know the secrets. I tell her the shapes, the signs, like I did with the cards and she nods, takes notes. Her notebook is purple, I notice, laugh. She's going to be purple in my brain from now on, a purple bruise. I remember you telling that blonde boy he was beautiful too. I tell Megan, the leaves are important but it's not about the leaves. It's about the way a person holds the cup. Read the angle of their wrist to see what they're hoping for, then tell them that. But that's not honest, Megan says, shocked. The bent parts of us, knees, elbows, wrists, knuckles, show everything we're wishing for by the lean in their bend. Megan wants me to be good, to do good, and to teach her to be good too. She thinks this is the same as having a life's purpose. It helps them to hear someone else say their wishes out loud, I tell her. It makes them feel real. You stood up and walked back to the bonfire with that blonde boy's arm around your waist. Left me looking up alone at the stars that refused to spin.

My husband walks out with me and the baby. We go to see the outsideman in his tent. We feel bad. Shame. He's got nothing and we've got everything. We did nothing to deserve this fortress. That's a beautiful baby, the outsideman says. And that's the way to get me to love you, tell me my baby is beautiful. Thank you, I say. My husband leans down closer to where the outsideman is sitting. This is the most humane thing about him, he gets close to people. Anyone. People on the streets, screaming. Drunk crying girls in party bathrooms open the door for him. Butterflies land on his nose. My husband looks the outsideman in the face and says, gently, how long are you planning on staying? The outsideman scratches his beard and looks at the sky. Have you seen the town down there?—he asks. No, we haven't. There's nothing left. This mountain is all there is. I thought your uncle would be here. I thought he'd take me in. I see, my husband says, standing up. I move with the baby towards the darkness of the forest. I want to walk in and see the deer with her baby. Listen for a bear. Be anywhere but near these human failures. Do you remember when that other girl wanted to be friends with us? We were thirteen, new animals, and she was lost and strange. No one liked her. We didn't like her. She had braces with multi-colored rubber-bands on her teeth. Fuck off, I told that girl, the first time I'd ever said it and meant it. I didn't want her contagion near me. I didn't want to be lonely and scared like she was. I reacted with force. You looked at me sideways, but you let the girl go. I don't think

40

you ever had any other friends but me. I wonder what made you so loyal. Even when I turned sixteen, got beautiful, and got swept up in all that beauty means. I wonder why you never told me to fuck off. I hope that girl is safe, but . . . THE CATASTROPHE—I see a skull with multi-colored rubber bands affixed to the teeth. Where are you going?–my husband calls to me. I've inched onto the paved trail into the forest. For a walk?–I ask. But, you're not wearing bug spray or sunscreen. I know, I tell him. We go anyway. We don't even tell my mother, her anxious face pressed to the kitchen window, that we're leaving. That we're walking the paved circle, that we'll be back, don't worry, don't worry. No bugs any more. We turn our backs on the outsideman as if to prove we're not afraid. Looking at my husband under the green light of the trees I realize this is why I fell in love with him. Him out of all the men. He's kind. Kind in his nature in a way I'll never be. He'd never react with teeth. He had all kinds of friends, didn't care what people said. And yeah, okay, I hear you, it's easier if you're a tall handsome man, it's safer, but still, he doesn't have to be kind. I reach out under the trees and take his hand. The baby squirms in her holder on my chest. The outsideman in the tent fades as the shadows get darker the deeper in the forest. We can't just let him live out there forever, my husband says. Where is he supposed to go?–I ask. Down the mountain. There's nothing down the mountain. We walk in silence, our palms sweaty. Then he tightens his grip on my hand and that's when I realize that the outsideman has made him afraid. For the first time, my husband bent his face down to the eyes of a suffering creature and recoiled at the risk he found staring back.

I REMEMBER THAT GIRL WITH THE MULTI-colored braces. I remember the hurt on her face like you'd sliced her with a knife no one could see. You're wrong, though. I wasn't angry with you or disappointed in your cruelty. I was proud. I thought it meant that you didn't want any other friends but me. A thirteen-year-old girl is possessive. I don't understand what you feel for this outsideman. Live inside. Listen to your husband. That's what you chose, so choose it. Well, maybe that's mean. Maybe I'm just yelling at the memory of you, your legs around that blonde-haired boy, saying he's so strong, as if strong was something everyone should be. Dog and I don't leave the trailer in the daytime. The sun roasts us. I've gotten good at stillness. I can sit at my fold-down Formica kitchen table and let the time pass on the horizon. I don't think I'll run out of food or water. What I'll run out of is time. I feel the small power pulsing in my palms. It wants to go out and fix a small thing, but instead, I sit and stare out my trailer's window at the sun's boiling progress over the desert sky. The girl with the colored markers came into my bed once and told me I was beautiful like the moon. Pale. Distant. She loved to compare me to things, the moon, that dead whale. It's like I existed as an image in relation to other images in her mind. I wasn't real until she drew on me. Red boats, green octopuses, blue houses with yellow roofs. But, I let her draw on me because she was small. So small I could have poured her into a teacup and the brim wouldn't well and spill. I thought that meant she couldn't hurt me. I thought that meant, when it came to it, I'd win in a fight. As I drove to the desert from the ocean, sitting still behind the wheel, even as my car was hurtling through space, I was thinking that I would like to spend the rest of my life staying more or less still. Megan won't come today. Dog will lay at my feet and do as I do. I'm his queen and he loves me in his Dog way, but the power imbalance isn't in his favor. I found him, right after I unloaded my one box of belonging into the trailer. He came walking out of the desert, collar loose around his bony neck. Someone had abandoned him. Someone didn't want to feed him anymore. I took him in because, you know, I can be sentimental sometimes. The love of a dog is better than no love at all. If I hadn't run away, if I'd gone to college like you did and read all the books that you read, do you think I'd be a different person? I wonder if I could have done something with the power pulsing in my palms. But, no. It's no good to think like that. I had to leave when I could. Now, the places to run to are burning up or flooding. Where do the weird kids dream of running away to now? The moon? I wonder where Megan will go when the time comes. Dog will stay at my feet. I think that no matter what happened when we were seventeen I was always going to end up here, and you were always going to end up there. I drink my tea in the heat and feel the leaves on my tongue. I don't need to read them to know what they'll say.

TWO

It is perhaps needless to say that they felt they had entered a dream, or a catastrophe, or simply a new life.

—Fleur Jaeggy, *Water Statues*

When we eat dinner, the lights on in the cabin obscure our view of the tent. My mother worries her pearls between her fingers. Should someone take food out to him? We pause. It's not that he's done anything. He hasn't. He hasn't done anything but lie in the sun and chew on his blade of green grass. The boys went running wild after a while and they said they heard him humming to himself, that's all. I think of what he said. The town is destroyed. THE CATASTROPHE is sinking strip malls into the ground. I'll take a plate to him, I say. My baby watches me. Sometimes I think her eyes are old. Do you remember that boy you pushed in the lake? How he raped that girl a year younger than us? They found her body in the water and the police thought he drowned her, but he said he'd raped her and left her alive in the mud. That girl had big blue eyes like my daughter. You should have drowned him, but I guess you'd have gone to prison if you did. I take the food to the outsideman. It's dark. Not near as buggy as it used to be, moths, lightning bugs, gnats everywhere. I used to think they were creepy—all those legs. Now I miss them. Remember our forest? Raising our sweaty hands above our heads because you said gnats congregate around our highest points? I give the outsideman his food and he thanks me. I look for the wolf in his eyes, but I don't find it. He seems gentle. I wonder where you ran off to when the rest of us went to college. I pictured you on a motorcycle, does that make you laugh? I pictured you in a leather jacket flipping off truckers. I wonder if you're in a tent somewhere like this man. I wonder if someone is handing you a plate of food. How are you feeling?–I ask the outsideman. Fine, he says. He says that he can hear the trees whispering to each other. He thinks we're out of the way of most of THE CATASTROPHE up here. But?–I ask. But, you never know, he says. There was once a small town Bait-and-Tackle, kayak rentals, now there is nothing, nothing. His father was a mailman, the outsideman says. He walked in those dorky shorts delivering mail for thirty years. Thirty years in the sun. Skin cancer took him. Took him before all this. I look over my shoulder and I can see my whole family, clear, in the light of the dining room. They're eating. My baby has her head turned towards me. Don't make me not exist. You're going to stay here?–I ask the outsideman and he says, I'm only one man, as if he's asking for a small thing. Well, let me know if you need a blanket or anything, I say. He's finished eating, so I take his plate.

He won't need a blanket, it's so hot outside. I wonder how the flowers pollinate themselves now. I think of the town, submerged by the lake. I think of the boy with the wolf eyes; you pushed him, sopping, you should have drowned him. There should have been consequences. I guess we're all facing those consequences now. I slide the glass door open and rejoin my family. They avoid my eyes. Shame. Why could you always see when everyone else was blind?

MEGAN COMES AT NIGHT. SHE HAS THE terrarium, Giles the gecko. She says her mother is freaking out. There're no more drugs for the junkies. The catastrophe has eaten up their supply chain. Her mother has scratched raw lines into her forearms. She wants to disappear, Megan says. She wants to scratch herself out of existence. Can I stay here?—Megan asks, but she's already thrown her backpack on the trailer floor. I set her up on my futon. Her limbs are like a baby deer. Sure, I remember the forest, the wolf-eyed boy, the gnats. Do you remember the yellow flowers we found growing from that deer's skull? And you said it was too on-the-nose. I give Megan a blanket. Dog whines. He wants to come inside. We're having a party without him. I open the door and he huffs onto the futon next to Megan. Sweet boy, she says, stroking his ears. His eyes shine with devotion. Dogs are so easy. People too. I ask her if she needs anything else. She asks me how I saved Giles the gecko. I just have it in me, I tell her. How? You're born with it, I say.

Then, for some reason, I don't know, loneliness? The novelty of hearing my voice speak out loud? I tell her about my mother. Things I never had to tell you. You were there. You saw her. How thin, how tired. Always tired, always aching. Migraines. Fatigue. How my house became a hushed, dark place. A tomb. How my father didn't believe her, thought she invented her pain for attention, like, look how fragile I am. How her hair fell out the summer we turned fifteen. Thick black clumps of hair like fur. It grew back wiry, gray, and brittle. That summer was the summer her voice got old. Crone. Don't be like me, she whispered. So that's why I was seeking colors. I did have a motorcycle, how could you have guessed that? I stole it. I stole it from a bar parkinglot and could have gotten killed for it, but it worked out. Nobody ever found me. Scott-free. Wind in my hair, flies in my teeth. Still so many flies back then. Tiny transparent wings. I tell Megan that I ran when I could and that I ended up with the girl who drew on my arms by the sea. Colorful markers, dead whale, but I could never outrun the image of my mother. The pain. In her bedroom. Quiet. My greatest fear. A tomb. You were with a woman? Megan asks, I mean *with* a woman? And I snort, sexuality's a spectrum, gender is a lie, Megan is young and supposed to know these things. But there's a church, I always forget, at the center of her town's clenched fist, and so I nod and I tell her I've always loved women a little bit more. Me too, Megan says, except for my brother. What about your man?–I ask, and she smiles into the futon, breathes in and out, the scent of Dog's fur. He doesn't love me, Megan says, but I need something to hold on to. I can see her man, in the echoing back of my mind. He's almost gone, almost like he was never there at all. There's a church

48

meeting tomorrow, Megan says, about killing ourselves if the rain doesn't come. Don't kill yourself, I tell her. My heart is afraid. I won't, she says, but I see her purple feet dangling. You should come to the church, she says. They'd burn me on the spot, I tell her, and she knows this, knows what their clenched fists do to a woman like me. But she laughs. I'd like to see them try, she says. Then laughs again. My mother is also a *disappointment,* she says, the word rolling around in her mouth like something sweet to eat.

After dinner, my husband and I sneak to our bedroom for alone time. It's embarrassing because the rest of the family knows what we're doing, has to watch the baby while we take care of our bodies. So we try to make it quick, which always makes me nervous. Different from when we were in our early twenties and could have sex anywhere, anytime, flexible, always ready. Once, we had loud messy sex in the concrete shower stall of a hostel in Amsterdam. Slippery. Back when people could still travel, vacation. Planes. Passports. I wonder if we'll ever vacation anywhere again. My husband is gentle, even though it's been a while because of all the worry and packing and heading to the store for supplies and guarding our provisions and getting out of town. It feels better than it did with my high school boyfriends, who were clumsy and didn't know they had to *do* anything to make me relax, make me enjoy it. After we're done, and it is quick release, but not embarrassingly so, we lie still, hoping to get a few more minutes alone, away from the family. Naked and warm and almost at peace. I can't help it, the thought is still biting my cheek with sharp teeth. I ask, do you really think that guy outside is dangerous? Over the years, because of his job, my husband has gotten used to foul human odors, the sweat, spit, mean words. He closes his eyes and says he's afraid, this time, he's afraid of this man. Maybe he's hit his limit on human compassion. He spent so much of his adult life in the dirt, trying to sweep it off of people, and what did it get him? THE CATASTROPHE. How many of his clients survived the fires? The gunshots? What difference did he make to them? I roll over and kiss his scruffy mouth. He grew a beard when we moved from school to the city for his job, said it made him look older. I've seen the fear in my husband's eyes. Seen him recoil from the outsideman in a way he never did from his mentally ill clients, homeless people on the street, drug addicts. You think he could hurt us?–I ask, remembering the outsideman's ropey muscles; he must know how to hunt and butcher animals because somehow he's survived. I don't know what to think anymore, my husband says, his beloved body curling around mine, his breath shallow in my ear. He's outside, I say. We'll see it if he tries anything. You're right, my husband says, and I can feel him drift off to sleep, his muscles finally relaxing, the first time in a long time. I rub circles on his back and try to rest too, but all I can think about is our patch of green and his red tent still there, like a bug bite or a sore.

AT LEAST, IN BED WITH YOUR HUSBAND, YOU stop thinking for a minute. How embarrassed would you be if you knew I could hear your thoughts of skin and tongue and legs and hair? I'm not jealous anymore. Even though it's been a long time for me since the girl with the multicolored markers. She made it exciting, our bodies like a tide, push and pull; she made it hurt. She made everything hurt and I liked it. I don't know now why I liked it so much. Maybe it was what I thought I deserved. But now I'm like a virgin oracle in Ancient Greek times; I can't sully my body if I want all this power. All this. Hah. Maybe I should start telling the people that come here the things that they don't want to hear. Things like—this is all your fault—which is something I never say. If I lay blame on them I'd have to accept blame too. But, now I think maybe I *could* accept it. Before, on my motorcycle or hiding in a dive bar, all shadows and sticky wooden surfaces, I thought I could hide from myself. Have you ever wanted to disappear like that? Back then, I'd give my body to anyone, grateful that they wanted it, happy to oblige. I see that impulse a little in Megan too. How she wanted to give herself to a man who didn't deserve her, a man who was using her as a warm placeholder, something to occupy

51

himself with until he tumbled on. Why do you think we accept these sorts of arrangements? You never did. You had that high school boyfriend and then casual sex, casual sweat, one adoring boy-man after another, you, tetherless, but free. How did you avoid throwing yourself into the fire of someone else's indifference? *You* were the fire. That's a power that you have and I don't. I respect that. You'd never get caught up in a desert doomsday church. Never need someone to tell you that soon, very soon, pretty soon, if you're good, it'll rain, things will get better, if you do as I say. Of course no one believes it, or I never did, but it felt good to follow something, felt so good to have someone say, *kneal,* say, *hurt yourself,* say, *it'll be worth it.* Was it because your parents loved each other more than mine did? Was it because you felt safer as a girl than I did? Wake up from your snooze and pulse a little power over to me, please. Let me have some of that resolve, so I can keep the church away from my trailer, so I can give a little to Megan, so she can stand up for herself. When they come for me I'll try to hold my head up high, ignore the way they look at me, the way they'll think, disgusted, *witch.* If you were here that's what you'd do, hold your head up. I know they'll come. Any day now.

My sister and mother are having a whispered fight at two in the morning. The cabin is dark and they think no one hears them, but I don't sleep. I listen to their voices, and I hear an irritated *whoosh whoosh hiss.* Fighting with little pockets of air. I get up, notice my husband's face caught in a moonbeam, smooth back his hair, kiss the mole on his forehead shaped a little like Flordia. My baby is sleeping. Deep, deep breaths. I walk to the hallway. What is it?–I whisper. Why the fighting? My mother and sister look at me like animals caught in the dark. Their eyes shine like spider eyes. We're afraid, they tell me, we want the outsideman gone. He's not doing anything, I say. He knew our uncle. He called my baby beautiful. But, they're worried that he's going to rise up while we're sleeping, that he has a machete secreted somewhere, that he will chop up the children in front of our eyes. You hear about things like that these days, my sister says. Massacres. No man is content sleeping in a tent in front of a house like this, my mother says. He wants what we have. I think about the paved trail, about how soon, without tending, it will become overgrown with weeds. So what are you going to do?–I ask them. How are you going to force him to go? We can't hurt him. He hasn't done anything but ask for help. You should go to sleep, my sister says. She sees in me some reluctance, some exhaustion. He's harmless, I say. Listen to your sister, my mother says, you should go back to sleep now. I know what I'm saying, my sister says, you should get some sleep while you can, sleep keeps your brain alive. And, maybe because they said sleep so many times, I close my eyes and sway, standing, for a second. I am so tired, I tell them. I know, my mother says. Sometimes, I forget, you know, because I'm so, so tired. That makes sense, my sister says, soothe, soothe, soother. They are like me. They have faces like mine. We all have the same nose, the same right foot that turns out like a duck. I smile. Okay, I say, I'll go to bed. That's good, my mother says. Yeah, good call, says my sister. I pull up our woods in my mind now. How alive the woods were with the noises of unseen things. I wasn't afraid, then, but I'm afraid now. It's like the constant hum of fatigue in my bones, fear, fear, fear. Remember the year your mother's voice turned old? I'll never forget the shock of her newly white hair. Maybe I'm worried that one day I'll wake up and my hair will be white like that and it will mean that I can never be touched again. I slide into bed next to my husband's warm body. I slip my hands along the bare skin of his hips. His eyelids lift. He smiles at me. I tug his boxer shorts down, tug my panties off. We have to be quiet, I whisper into his mouth. We're barely awake when our bodies slide together, but it feels good. Even better than before, more natural, spontaneous. Twice in one day. I'm no crone. The calm night, the blue night, the *hush hush hush* of the night. I fall asleep in my husband's arms and I forget why I woke up at all.

IN THE MORNING, MEGAN IS STILL ON THE futon. She sleeps like a child, her limbs thrown everywhere. Babies sleep like that, hands raised in surrender. I creep out of the trailer to take a piss in the desert. Dog stays by Megan's side, he loves her. Maybe dogs are chumps, suckers for scraps of kindness, or maybe they're the best judges of character. I walk out, my toes in the sand. The desert heat, even at dawn, scalds my heels. Remember when heat would come and go? When fear would ebb and flow? I feel that fear like a buzzsaw, too. It shakes my bones. I take a piss watching the sun rise. When I turn around Megan is standing outside watching me. I'm not embarrassed. She should know that some of the rumors about me are true, sometimes I'm filthy. Do you have food?–she asks when I walk back to her. I buried most of it a long time ago, I say. Where?–she asks, but I tap the side of my nose like we're in a heist movie. It's best if only I know, I say. Food is getting scarce in the desert. People kill for food. I heard that there was a fire in the old Super Walmart. The horizon choked with smoke told me. Hungry people ransacked the shelves and then they burned down the store's shell out of spite. It had nothing left to sell. Nothing left worth stealing. Come on, I have eggs, I tell her. It's a rare thing to have eggs out here, but I know a lady with a chicken. How she keeps it alive is beyond me. The thing must be skin and bones, but she still lays, hoping something will hatch. The woman gives me eggs in return for having her future told. Even though her future is like all of ours: death, rebirth, change, death. She sighs with relief when I tell her that, because all she fears is stillness. Stasis. Megan's eyes get wide, but I'm not lying, I have eggs. She watches me make them, like eggs are all that my magic is. She asks, why do you piss in the desert? I laugh. Dog perks his ears. Because I can, I tell Megan and she smiles. Of course I remember laying on our backs in the woods, listening to the noises of unseen things. I could tell which were friend and which were foe, but you never could. Everything sounded like an enemy. I don't like the hissing sound of women whispering in the dark. Megan's canines are yellowing. There's hardly any toothpaste anymore. I put the eggs on a plate for her and she eats like a dog. Slobber. It makes me laugh. She's filthy too. You know you could go somewhere else, I tell her. She looks at me, sad. I can't leave my mother. Not after my father and my brother. But, she's left you, I say. Every time she shoots up, she leaves you. She's going to get clean, Megan says. She's got no choice. The drugs are drying up. The drugs will be the last thing to go, I say. You sure you won't come to church? I'm sure. Megan thanks me for the eggs. She turns on my little kitchen faucet and scrubs at her freckled face until it's pink. I've got to be clean for church, she says. I've got a shower, I say, but she laughs—too small. Can I leave Giles here?—she he asks me and I say sure, why not? There's going to be a woman coming by later, I can taste her on the dust coming in on the wind. A woman who's on her way to the city. To irrigated parks, trees hemmed in by concrete, amenities or what's left of them. She's just got one question for me. Do you know the answer?—Megan asks and I nod, of course, of course Giles can stay. I'll come get him once church is over, Megan says, once I'm sure my mother is still alive. You can come and go as you please, I say, although I'm not sure why I say it. I'm a door that swings open and shut too easily. Do you remember my father's face, yelling yellow spittle on the front lawn, telling me to get the hell out? That's the night I stole the motorcycle. The last night I ever saw you. Maybe one day, before this is all over, you'll hear my voice in your head. Can I stay forever?—Megan asks, but she's out the door before I can say yes again.

I wake in the middle of the night. I can't seem to make my body sleep the whole night through anymore. When I was a child, I had fantastic dreams. I could fly, breathe fire. Now all my dreams are about my teeth falling out, or an elevator dropping with me inside, or forgetting something, something essential, that hurts the people I love. Staring at the stucco ceiling, I think of my mother. Her pearls. She grew up in the city back when the city was just another catastrophe for poor people. She didn't have enough to eat. She got beat up in the girl's bathroom at school by tough girls who thought she was a snob. She who is a a snob now, who never shows her fear, was once a child like we were once children. And then she met my father, who strolled so easily into the comfort of a house, of food, of safety, leading her by the hand. She ordered his life. Of all of us, my uncle liked my mother best. He said she had ambition, but what I think he meant was hunger. And now she wants to pretend, now that THE CATASTROPHE has spread to everyone, that she never elbowed a girl in the nose, blood running down her sleeve, to survive. That she never got in a car with an older man, who might have murdered her, might have done anything and gotten away with it, just to feel like she mattered. When she met my father she had a purpose. Order. Young women need a purpose. And what's mine? Now that I have the baby it's easy to say that she's my purpose, protecting her, but isn't that too much to put on her shoulders? Isn't that too heavy a burden for a baby? But, I bet that's what my mother would say. That I'm her purpose. Me and my sister and all of us, even the cat. Protecting us. Accepting whatever she needs to accept in order to keep us safe. I imagine her elbowing the outsideman in the face. Blood running down her sleeve. There goes the cartilage in his nose. She wouldn't even feel bad about it. And should she? I roll over and watch my husband sleep. Tall man safe. He lives a thousand miles away from his mother. A frail woman—sad. We haven't been able to contact her since THE CATASTROPHE started. Maybe she's dead. Maybe she starved or burned or wasted away—her purpose spent. I close my eyes and try to dream of green fields, but I see you standing there—big stick covered in blue green lichen—ready to fight. I pick up my own stick and swing it overhead.

I DON'T WORRY ABOUT MY MOTHER. SHE'S
dead and nothing can hurt her. Do you think your mother
is wrong? Do you think she should let other people beat her
up, take things from her, just on principle? Was it wrong for
her, more beautiful than anyone else's mother, to grab your
father and ride him to the suburbs? I think of dust when I'm
alone, now. I think of silent dust. I try to curl up into a silent
place inside my chest, but like a hermit crab using a glass
bottle as a shell the dust swirls around me like grains in an
hourglass, all the voices, and I can spend whole days watching
everything fall. Isn't that some sort of zen accomplishment?
Aren't I like a monk, The Hermit, devoted to meditation and
compassion? It's getting harder to do, to come back, that's
why I've let Megan in. Even Dog, even Giles, a tiny spotted
lizard, anything to bring me back to the real. I want to protect
them all—a dangerous impulse. It's funny that you're trying
to protect everyone also. That you think, with a little violence,
you can keep your family safe. What about the forest fires?
What about another virus? Who are you going to elbow in
the nose to keep those things at bay? Sometimes I think of
my father. His tortoiseshell glasses. The mole on his chin. In
some ways he is the most real person in the world to me. A
sea-green cardigan with a moth hole on the right shoulder
seam. Reading his books of war. God, he loved Winston
Churchill. Bulldog in a bowler hat. The same impulse, I

think, as your mother. The desire to protect those we love. Where can we send the tanks? Who can we shoot? To keep catastrophe at bay. What to do, then, when your son, your daughter, turns out to be the threat? Where to point your gun then? I never knew why my mother married him. They never made sense to me as a couple the way your parents did. Your parents, at least, looked like they had sex—sorry—like they *liked* to have sex with each other. My parents must have had sex once, of course, because duh, here I am, an uneasy mix of them both, but I remember my mother recoiling from my father's every touch. She said his hands were too cold. Was it all the war books? All the voices of the valorous, glorious dead boys whispering his inadequacy? All the duststorms in his head. If he's still alive—I don't hear him, but maybe he is—whose side is he on now?

In the morning it is: bustle, feed the baby, pour cereal, oat milk, rub eyes, drink coffee, kiss my husband's morning-stale lips. It is: pull up a chair for my brother-in-law, ruffle the heads of my cranky nephews, tell my father that today we should all go for a walk in the woods, that it's important for my parents' old knees that they keep walking. It is so much noise, the radio, THE CATASTROPHE, the static, the classical music, that it takes me two hours to realize that the outsideman's tent is gone. He's gone, I say. Nobody looks up from their cereal. My husband frowns. Did he move into the woods? I don't know, he's gone, I say. Good riddance, says my sister. I feel a slow kind of fear rise in my stomach, apprehension, like I know something bad is going to happen. Maybe it has already happened. Your mother thought she could move small objects with her mind, I think most girls think they have a magical power, or wish they had one, buried, weak, under their diaphragms. Mine would be to know when danger has winged overhead. Is winging. Hawks, feathers, talons, beaks, danger, something has swooped and plucked the tent from the earth. Do you think he's okay?—I ask. Of course he's okay, my mother says, a bite in her voice. She says, We're the only ones up here. The town is burned out, THE CATASTROPHE got him. He must have moved on, my brother-in-law says. He must have moved deeper into the woods. I try to imagine this is true. I try to imagine the outsideman becoming a tree, gnarled bark, mossy beard. I say, Well should we look for him? Why?—my sister asks and I can't come up with a reason. There is no reason I should go looking for the outsideman. My husband reaches over and squeezes my hand. He likes that I feel bad. That I think maybe the man has fallen into a deep dark hole and that if I don't go searching for him he'll never be found. Then, it is: wash the bowls, brush your teeth, brush your hair, put on clothes. My sister calls down from her second story bedroom. We should go for a walk! We should all go for a walk in the woods! It's the first time she's suggested an outdoor activity. I think about the food we have in the pantry. The dozens upon dozens of cans, pasta, fruits, vegetables, preserved. Unperishable. I think about the moments of THE CATASTROPHE broadcast before my mother could turn the dial. There are fires burning. Diseases. Rot. Decay. Sure, I call up the stairs. The woods! Remember when your mother told me she could move objects with her mind, but they were too small to matter? I told her it was still beautiful, her gift, even if it didn't seem to affect anything at all, maybe it still had an effect, a butterfly effect. My husband asks me to spray bug spray on his neck and his ankles. The bugs are almost gone. I spray, breathe in the chemicals, remember how you rolled your eyes at your mother that year her voice got old.

I WATCH GILES IN HIS TERRARIUM. HIS STICKY toes press into his glass. He licks his eyeball. Does he know he's going to live longer than any gecko ever should? That he's a little abomination? The thought makes me fond of him, even if I imagine his skin is slimy and carries disease. I'm an abomination too, I whisper. Do you really think your outsideman just walked into the woods? Do you think he just decided, on his own, to leave? The woman I tasted on this morning's wind pulls up sooner than I expected her to. She's got an SUV, the kind I haven't seen in ages. Gleaming black in the sun. Tinted windows. Exhaust fumes. Real fuel. I can see boxes of stuff piled in the back when she opens the door. I can taste the petroleum tang of her air conditioner on the dust she kicks up. Hey, she says, like we're friends. Maybe she knows that I expect people before they come. Hey, I say. Listen, I don't believe in magic or anything, she says, straight off. She wants me to know she's no sucker, but her expensive sunglasses scream otherwise. I tilt my head to the side, the spring in my neck makes me feel like Giles. If I could lick my own eyeball now to freak this lady out, I would. Come inside, I tell her. She sits at the kitchen table across from me. Giles in between us. I don't explain. You're escaping to somewhere? I ask. THE CATASTROPHE will be over eventually, she says. It's just a matter of holding on. Holding on to what?—I ask. She reaches up and puts her sunglasses on her head. They stare, opaque, at me from the top of her hair. Hold on to who we used to be. Oh, I say, who did you used to be? She sighs. She says, listen, I don't believe in any of this, okay? I'm not some stupid girl. She's got bangles on her wrists. Giles turns his gecko head toward her, regards her with an ancient reptilian gaze. I don't answer her protestations, too much. She doesn't believe in magic, but she drove that shiny car past the burned-down Super Walmart. She peered through her tinted windshield at the megachurch in a wildflower field. She kicked up dirt and dust and coughed and rubbed her nose red, all to get to me. Okay, I say. Silence gets them usually. She just wants information. Everyone wants information, I say, thinking of Megan burrowing into the red dust congregation. Waiting for rain. Thinking of her mouth open, of her red throat open singing, what exactly, at the sky? The thing is I'm going to meet someone in the city, the woman says. He's got a wall behind which we can hide. Should I kill him?—she asks. Before he kills me? That's the question they all ask in the end, birth, change, death, rebirth, death, change. I remember when you told my mother her power was beautiful. It made me jealous that you'd never said that to me. And why, *unbidden this thought,* couldn't she use her power to protect me? You should kill him, I tell her because that's the right answer. We are all just rabbits waiting for knife points in the dark.

This is what we do now, we walk in the woods. My father stretches out his old knees. My mother sighs and puts her palm on the small of her back. The boys bounce ahead, stick-swords aloft. My baby stares out from the carrier strapped to her father's chest. My sister talks about the radio. She heard on the radio that THE CATASTROPHE will recede soon, like a tide. That it will wash out and pull back, exposing dead bodies and crumbling buildings and bones, but that life will grow there again. She says she thinks she could still get a job. She works in the financial sector and there will always be rich people who need their money moved around. It's not receding, my brother-in-law says. He listens to a different kind of radio. Late at night, hushed like whispers, he presses his ear to big round speakers. The end has come, his radio says. The end has been waiting on the edges of our lives for longer than we realize. His kind eyes are hardening because of those whispers. He's started counting our rations, double-checking, planning ahead. That's doomsday nonsense, my sister says, pulling her hair back into a ponytail. She used to have a professional bob. Now, her hair is as long as it was when we were children. When she threw parties ,when my parents were away, snuck out of the house, and bought contraband Mike's Hard Lemonade with an unconvincing fake ID. Back then she stuck pictures of men she liked on her closet door. She cut men's heads out of magazines. It's not doomsday nonsense, her husband says. His eyes are on the boys, running loops, crashing through the underbrush, whooping. They say everything is going to change, he tells us. It's all collapsed. They say that the systems we're used to relying on don't exist anymore. Who's they?—my mother wants to know. Who's so important they put themselves on the radio? I look at the paved path under my feet. It makes me think of the paved road around that lake. Remember when my high school boyfriend told you that your eyes freaked him out? He said you had witch eyes. You said thank you. I loved him like a bad vodka shot. Shivers up and down my nerves. You, always pulling an ugly face, but wanting more, wanting to be drunk. They always say it's the end of the world, my sister says. Every generation wants to be special. There must have been an orange bulldozer that came through here once, a paver, something, whatever they call the truck that lays down the road. I would have known, once; my red-haired nephew was obsessed with trucks for years. Now THE CATASTROPHE leaves rusted-out trucks in its wake. Burned out Dollar Generals. No more army to command.

Things will go back to the way they were, my sister says, believing in the bright, hard edge of her morning radio. We'll see, says her husband. I keep my eyes open, looking left and right for a scrap of red fabric, the outsideman's tent hidden in the brush.

THE WOMAN LOOKS AT ME LIKE I'VE SLAPPED her. What do you mean I should kill him?–she asks. Yes, I remember your high school boyfriend. I don't blame him saying that I had witch eyes. I do. He's not wrong. I narrowed them at him and watched his pupils dilate. Isn't that the answer you came here for?–I ask her. She's not sure anymore. She wants something from this man she's going to see in the city. Something more than a pile of stuff. Something more than an SUV with tinted windows and climate control. Love? The thought makes me dizzy. I guess you love your baby. Do you love your husband? Your sister? What is it, even, to love? I try to think of it, try to feel it in my body, but all I can see is my father's red face, spittle on his lips, saying you never come back here, you never come back. Wasn't I his baby? I don't know, the woman says, now that it's come to it, I'm not sure that I have it in me to kill anyone. What will he do to you when you get to the city?–I ask. What's the city like? The city is full of people with dead cars, dead music, garbage, heat, chemicals, she says . . . *change, rebirth, death, change.* She doesn't say that last part; I add it in my head. So, why are you going? Because if something new is going to come out

66

of this, it's going to be there. If something new is going to come out of this, then I'm going to retreat to my childhood home. I thought about doing that before I bought the trailer in the desert. I thought about our cul-de-sac overgrown with vines. I thought about your eyes filled with tears saying, that boy was an idiot, clutching your stomach, saying, what am I going to do? I'll live in the ruin of my mother's house. I'll dress myself in those vines. It takes me a moment to shake that vision from my mind. Then, don't kill him?–I ask the woman. She snorts. Listen, I say, I don't know what you want from me. If you want me to tell you that no matter what you choose you're forgiven, then fine. I forgive you. Okay, says the woman, leaning her head down level with Giles' terrarium. She taps her pointer finger on the glass. Giles regards her with lazy disdain. You're the last stop for all of us going to the city, she tells me. What do you mean?–I ask. There's a bar, south of here. It's a grungy place. Full of murder. Rape. But, somebody wrote your name on the women's bathroom mirror. It's in Sharpie; it won't ever come off. A little map showing how to get to your place from there. Who would do that?–I ask. Purple Sharpie, she says, and suddenly I know. You're like a dead whale. Resurfacing, resurfacing. What does the mirror tell you about me?–I ask. It says that you'll have an answer. You read omens, the lonely flights of birds, the strange pull of tides. It says you know the best direction to run when things start to crumble. I don't run, I tell the woman. She smiles and fiddles with the bangles on her wrist. Then what are you doing here?

I don't see his tent in the bush even though I'm on the lookout during our entire family walk. And then, for the rest of the day, I forget about it. We're all too close together, in each other's way, in each other's hair. My sister and my mother are low-grade fighting without words. Psychic tension. The radio switched on, switched off, switched on. Doom. Hope. Doom. My husband is flipping through a picture book with my daughter on his lap. We have nothing but time. Time together with the dogs and the cat. The three of them have formed an unlikely pack. I thought the cat would be eaten the first day, but she seems to rule over the dogs with cool indifference. They want to please her. She washes her paw. It makes me think of you in high school. How you went cool overnight, badass, because you pushed that guy into the lake. How people whispered about you, wondered about you. About what else your hands could do. Do you remember the squirrel you prodded with a stick that lept back up, but I swear it was dead. Like, there were flies in its eyes. I remember your father's face that time. . . . The dogs make rounds from front door to back door, their ears perked. They're on the lookout for danger that never comes. The cat snoozes, eyes closed, unconcerned with all of us, unconcerned with the world. My baby points a finger at the page. Her father kisses her head. My mother says, why don't they play music on the radio anymore? Stop all this talking and play some music. I think about the folder that explained my uncle's money. I decide I don't want to dig into it any more. What were his options? Oil? Pharmaceuticals? Investments? I don't want to know. I turn a blind eye. What can I do? Me and my baby and this family? Can we prod a squirrel with a stick and bring it back to life? Do you think we're going to drive each other crazy?—my brother-in-law asks me. I listen to the dogs' nails *click click* on the cabin floor. This is what a medieval fortress feels like. We were supposed to have evolved beyond such fortifications. We never did. We're already crazy, I tell my brother-in-law. The boys are being quiet, for once. They wore themselves out in the woods, whooping for blood. I never saw the outsideman's tent, red on the horizon. I wonder, if you were here, what would you see? I turn my head and stop thinking like that. The dogs at the door bare their teeth, but it's only a lone robin, red-breasted on the grass, hopping where it belongs.

MEGAN COMES BACK FROM CHURCH. DOG AND I are still on the floor. She looks clean, smells like soap, high neckline, pastel dress, two swinging braids. She lays down head to head with me, feet pointing in different directions. Dog snuffles at her nose, she wrinkles it, laughs. How was church?–I ask. There are tire marks in the sand outside, she says. I don't want to say, but I don't want to lie. It feels like Megan has a right to the truth. A lady came to ask about the future. Megan pulls the tip of one of her braids into her mouth and sucks. Hmm, she says. Church was fine, frenzied, people crying, rocking, shouting. My mother was there. How's your mother? My mother said she's clean, said she's never going to take drugs again, but I don't believe her. She was too calm to be clean. Serene. She was high. Where'd she get drugs? I think the pastor has a stash. I think he uses it to lure women. My mother's eyes followed him the entire time. He has stamina. Hands in the air for an hour, shouting about the wrath of God. What if he's right?–I ask. About what? About the wrath of God. What if God is wrathful? Megan sucks on her braid, thinks, closes her eyes. Maybe He is, she says. My ex-girlfriend wrote my location on a bathroom mirror, that's how these people are finding me. Megan laughs, Why? She had ideas about who I was supposed to be, I say. Above us, Giles is silent in his terrarium. Was it better?–Megan asks, being with a woman? That's a stupid question, I tell her. She shrugs. I can tell she's still thinking about her mother. It makes Dog anxious. Her mother's serene eyes, wet, following the doomsday pastor. Does the pastor mean what he says?–I ask. He means it, oh, he means it. Do you think it will rain? No, never again. Outside and around us the desert stretches on for miles and dusty miles. Red, red, alone, lifeless. No more scorpions, no beetles, no bugs now. I remember my mother dancing naked at your parents' party. I remember how angry it made my father, and how strong she seemed. I, too, am afraid that my strength will snap one day, in half, like hers did, clean. That I'll wake up and my head will hurt. What's the point of looking young? What's the point of growing old? In her church clothes, Megan looks like a child. She is thinking and I can hear her thinking. She's trying to figure out a way to keep her mother from dying, but there is no way. Sometimes it's best to just lay on the floor. Getting over his agitation, Dog huffs down on top of us. His weight pushes us into the floor. We smell like Dog. Megan doesn't move, doesn't seem to notice the heat of him. We can stay like this, a woman-dog pile. Don't kill yourself, I say. Megan blinks, nods. We can stay like this forever. Or, until the heat melts us or until the rain comes.

The way time passes, up here on the mountain, is different from how it passed below. In the city. Worry. My husband going out to the homeless shelter, the houseless, trying to get people housed. The people in the streets. THE CATASTROPHE. Their eyes, yellow. Their teeth. Their hands. I was afraid, even as I despised myself for that fear. My neighbor, Karen, knocking on my door, saying, Sugar for your neighbor? and I knew she was on drugs, so I kept the door shut, so then Karen just sat in the hallway, a measuring cup in her hand, and told me all about her boyfriend Bernard who'd been dead for years but was the one man who was ever kind to her. Up here on the mountain thoughts of Karen, her crispy bleached hair, her empty measuring cup, catch me unaware again. She'll pop into my head whenever I'm off guard because she was the first person I knew who was dead of THE CATASTROPHE. Heat stroke, they said. Bad diet, no money, a virus, mice in the walls. The mice ate her eyes. I hate that I know that, but it was in the paper. The mice ate the eyes out of her dead body. Cup of sugar for your neighbor? Before we moved up to the mountain, the cooler air, the breeze, my husband and I were always talking about moving. Move where? Anywhere. Somewhere cooler, no mice. Somewhere without people. That was the dream. Beautiful nature and no people. People made THE CATASTROPHE, we said, as if we weren't people, as if we didn't count. I make a lot of the food in the cabin. It's what I'm good at. Loaves of bread, pots of chili. I'm in charge of making sure the food lasts. Lasts how long? Years, we could stay up here for years if we wanted to. My brother-in-law double checks our hoard when he's feeling anxious. He counts the bags of rice and relaxes. My husband seems less worried now. Cup of sugar for your neighbor? The fresh air and isolation has been good for the purple half-moons under his eyes. I wonder if you touched Karen on her fish-belly forehead while she sweated out the pills, if she would have come to the other side clean. But, my baby is growing up here and I can't deny that it's been good for her. She's stronger, bolder. She doesn't let her cousins push her around. The three of them, a little pack, remind me of the two dogs and the cat. The boys want to make my baby laugh. They feel like they've accomplished something if they get her to smile. I could send my baby down the mountain when she turns eighteen, sword strapped to her back, cousins by her side, to build up a new world. Cup of sugar? The neighbors on the other side of us died next. They had a baby. Don't think about it. Gunshot wounds to the head. Despair. You could have touched them, maybe, or maybe your power is too small. In the morning, my husband kisses me and my baby puts her small hand in mine. I feel gratitude squeeze my intestines; it's almost painful. I think of the city apartment block where we used to live, overgrown, weeds, dead bodies, THE CATASTROPHE, and then us, alive, on our mountaintop.

MEGAN'S MOTHER DIED—OVERDOSE. MEGAN found her body, rigid and blueish, cold to the touch. She went to check after her mother didn't show up to church and found her body on the bed. She didn't look like she was sleeping. In church that day, the pastor said that water was a sacred thing, and a sign of God's blessing. His words echoed in Megan's head as she ran her fingers over her mother's dead face. If they were strong, if they did right, then the rain would come. Megan touched her mother's blue lips. If rain didn't come, that meant that God wanted the congregation to destroy itself. Megan's mother was ahead of the plan. Chasing numbness until numbness was all she had. Megan dragged herself to the trailer and sobbed on all fours like an animal. Nothing she could do, no violence could protect her mother from the needle. I wrapped my arms around Megan's shaking body until she quieted a little. Alone now. Father disappeared, brother dead, mother dead. Megan and Giles and me and Dog, a ragtag pack. I pulsed a little light into her forehead so she would sleep. I hoped she would dream nice dreams, or else have no dreams at all. Pulsing the light made me tired so we slept on the futon, my arms wrapped around Megan to make sure that she wouldn't crawl off and make good on her preacher's promise. Now, fierce as a grappling hook, I will have no quiet in me ever again. Instead, I will have to keep Megan safe. Safe from catastrophe, safe from herself. The weight of it, almost unbearable. Is this what it's like for you when you look at your baby? When we woke up, Megan guided me to the collapsed ranch house where her mother's body lay fetid in the heat. We dragged her to the congregation who huddled around the bloated corpse making sour faces; overdose was shameful, even at the end of the world. The preacher thanked me and told me I could join the church and stay, or refuse and go. His eyes said, *witch*. I refused but I crept just out of sight; I wasn't going to let them take advantage of Megan's grief. Who knows what they would make her do. She, wild-eyed, watched me go, her mouth open in a silent scream. I put my finger to my lips to let her know I wouldn't go far. The congregation took all day to bury her mother. Long-sleeved women dug a slow hole in the sucking sand. They wrapped her and sang songs and the preacher said it was a shame. To lose yourself in oblivion is a shame, the pastor said, as if oblivion wasn't what he preached every day. Sweat rolled in a torrent off his bald head and soaked his white shirt. Where did she get the drugs, man of God? They threw her mother's body in a hole in the desert. No different than any other hole in the desert. No marker, no graveyard. Megan's brother, at least, had a real funeral when he died, in a real cemetery. Then eerie singing started. It made me want to run but I hovered on the edges hiding behind a blackened dumpster they'd rolled down from the old Super Walmart parking lot. I listened to their voices curl up to the sky like smoke. When they left one by one, Megan collapsed on her knees in the dust. They left her there while the sun went down, alone against a sky red as blood. Now I put a hand on Megan's shaking shoulder. It's okay, I tell her because that's what you say when something evil has happened. I thought I could stop her, Megan says, her voice steady and sad. Come on, I say, and I lead her through the dark lit by stars—back to the silver trailer. Dog hears us coming and bounds out to Megan. He licks her hands, salty with tears. I lead her inside. I lead her home.

I watch the deer from inside the cabin. They come every morning now that they know we won't hurt them. They bend their necks in the high grass where the outsideman's tent once was. I see him in scraps. He had a beard? He seemed strong? His tent was red. I laid down on a carpeted floor with my husband before he was my husband. We were both young and in our first apartment and my parents said, don't worry about the damp, the mould, the mice, the money. Everything comes with time. That was one of my mother's favorite sayings. Everything comes with time. It sounds sinister now. She doesn't say it anymore. On the carpet, dirty, covered in the dirt of other renter's feet, my husband, who was just my boyfriend then, a boy, lanky, kissed my forehead and said—it's the beginning. We thought it was. We thought we'd start here in our basement and work our way up. That summer the heavy rains started and the basement flooded. The management pulled up our carpet and put industrial fans underneath it to dry it out. It didn't work. We were damp for months. I felt like mould was going to grow out of my fingers. I'd wake up one day, green and fuzzy, more like moss than like a person. It's a step, my husband said when we moved up a floor, but the floods didn't stop coming. There was a squirrel who'd been tamed by an old man down the apartment block. It climbed down out of its tree and waited for him on the bench. He used to feed it nuts. Its hands looked too much like human hands. When the old man died the squirrel waited for him on the bench. Other residents took pictures of the squirrel with their phones. How cute! He sits like a person! All of this feels like decades ago but it wasn't. When the real floods came and the winds, I guess that squirrel died with all the others. How long do squirrels live? Even the ones we imbue with human longing? Now I'm surrounded by the ghosts of dead squirrels. Everywhere the trees rustle. We are never alone. We go for walks and it is green, green isolation and then a red tent in my mind, but when I turn it's never real. My baby grows like a weed. She says, Mama, and I can feel my heart bleeding inside my chest. My mother and sister fight, declare truce, fight, declare truce. We live in a permanent state of detente. The radio says it's worse at the foot of the mountain. The floods are worse and the electricity is out. THE CATASTROPHE. We don't even say the words anymore. No one else, besides the outsideman, has tried to come up the mountain. We are safe in our isolation. I bake bread and stir the pot. Do you remember the chapel connected to our middle school? Do you remember the big dead Jesus? How you looked up at him and felt, not even pity, nothing? You said he knew he was going to heaven so what kind of sacrifice was it? I said, it must have hurt a lot at the time. But now I see your point, sometimes, listening to the radio static, hearing my brother-in-law mutter that it's the end of the damn world.

I HEAR YOU IN WAVES NOW, AS TIME PASSES more quickly. I feel like the Earth is spinning faster. The stars wheel overhead faster. Megan is starting to learn things. Once, she told a pilgrim who was here to see me that her future was stamped on her forehead. What is it?–the pilgrim asked; she had lilac-colored hair (I wonder where she'd found the dye.) It's death, rebirth, change, death, Megan said, and I laughed out loud, *bark*, because she sounded so much like me. Her freckles turned rosy with pleasure. That's what we tell all the pilgrims and in exchange they give us stuff. One gave us a six-pack of beer. I hadn't had a beer in ages; Megan had never had one. We went out into the desert, Dog close at Megan's heels, and stared up at the sky, drinking. Tell me more about the woman with the multi-colored markers, Megan said. She wasn't very nice, I said. Megan nodded, waited; I drank the beer, wished and waited to feel fuzzy, felt it in my fingertips, a little. She said I was like a dead whale, once, I said. Megan laughed. Seriously? Yeah, it was dead on the beach where we lived. You lived at the beach? Once. So, why'd you move here? I was hoping to be alone, I said. Megan frowned up at the stars. As the lights below flicker out one by one, the stars above us grow grander in scale. I feel like I can taste them, like licking the end of a battery, spark. You know I haven't heard from my man in ages, Megan said. So then is he still your man?—I asked. I knew he wasn't. I knew he was shacked up with his redhead, that he'd forgotten to text Megan goodbye. I wanted a man to help me, Megan said. I wanted a man to serve. You think that's what the church is? A man to serve?—I asked. Megan frowned. She'll learn all I'll teach her about cards and foretelling the future, but she doesn't like it if I start to poke holes in her theology. They say it's going to rain by the end of this month, Megan said. They said that two months ago. Megan opened her third beer and pointed up at the sky. It's going to be so beautiful when we're gone, she said. I've got plenty of food, relax, I said. Yeah, but, eventually, Megan stared at the sky, stars in her eyes, it'll be so beautiful when it's alone. You thinking of moving to the city?—I asked her. I've noticed the notes she keeps about the paths the migrants were taking. I wondered if she were making a map. I remember the big dead Jesus, how he stirred nothing in me, not even pity. You know what will never leave me? That whale. But sad-eyed Jesus, covered in blood and soon to be king, was that real pain? When you knew there was infinite power at the end of it? No, Megan said. I'll stay here. But there's nothing here, I told her. There's my mother's grave, my brother's grave, Megan said, tilting her head back. I watched the beer pour into her throat. And there's you and the stars, she said. We looked up together.

I saw it after I stopped looking for it. Isn't that how it goes? When I was trying to get pregnant, women told me that all the time. Relax. Like my body couldn't conceive because of stress. If that was true, there'd be no wartime babies. My baby came looked-for. I waited for her for a long time. This snuck up on me, a flash of color in the woods. We walk in the woods every morning, every evening, any time just to get out of the house. The circle trail, paved, shows no sign of cracking, but it will one day. One day I'll see a crack. It snuck up on me during a morning walk. Baby strapped to my back, husband at my side. He was pointing up at the trees, telling me which kind were which kind based on the shapes of their leaves. When all the people die, will there even be different kinds of trees? Green, green, green. Everything is green longer now. Then, winter is shockingly white. Biting cold in a way it never used to bite. But, for now, green everywhere. Green shoots, green leaves, even the light is green. Then, a flash of red. Like blood spilled on the floor. Wait, I told my husband. What? What's that? It's nothing, he called over his shoulder, but the baby and I walked off the trail. A big gnarled tree, the kind that has whorls in the trunk that look like faces and behind it, there, a slice of red in the green light. I reached down and grabbed the red by the corner, pulled. Leave it!–my husband said, but I didn't leave it. I pulled and yanked, my baby's feet knocked into my back, until I'd pulled out all the red from the earth. Covered in muck, rotted leaves and dirt, the red was blotchy brown in some places, but it was unmistakable. The outsideman's tent. What does this mean?–I asked, looking up at my husband. He frowned. He hadn't wanted me to pull it out of the earth. Maybe he'd noticed it before I had and had made a choice not to see it, not to disturb it. I don't know, he said. You think he left it here?–I asked, but even then it sounded wrong. Why would he leave his tent? Where would he sleep? I don't know, my husband said. We didn't turn around and go back to the cabin. We kept on the circular route. I thought it over. Maybe he found something better?–I asked. Maybe he found someone to take him in? The trees around us were silent and green. My husband stopped pointing at the leaves. I don't know, he said, but it's not good. When we got back to the cabin and told my family what we'd seen, they looked down at their feet. It doesn't mean anything, my mother said. It made me think of unburying things. Remember how, when you showed your father who you were, he turned red as the tent and threw you out? Remember how, when your mother died, they lowered her softly into the ground. What do you mean, it doesn't mean anything?–I asked. My mother pressed her mouth into a firm straight line.

MEGAN FINALLY MADE HER MOVE TO BE WITH me. I'd had the feeling for a while that she wanted to be something like my wife. An old kind of wife, a frontier wife, who took orders and did hard chores. I woke up and she was topless, sitting in my bed like she was a fruit basket with a bow on it. Hey, she said. No, I said. Her face fell right down to the floor, and then I felt bad. It's not that she isn't pretty in a plain desert dust kind of way. She'd look like an oil painting if she ever put on a bonnet. It's not that you're not pretty, I said, when she put her shirt back on. The back of her neck was red and she wouldn't look at me. Yeah, right, she said. It's not! It's just that . . . you don't have to be that way with someone for them to look after you. Megan lifted her head at that, looked me in the eyes. I can look after you too, she said. I know, I said. I contribute, she said. You do, sure you do, I said. I'm just too old for all that now. I thought it was better than telling her that she was too young. You're not old, she said, laughing. I was young before the catastrophe, I said. Anyone who was young before the catastrophe is old now. I've only ever known the catastrophe, Megan said. So I guess I'll never be old. I laughed, got up, got us water, cool. She said, I'll be your wife anyway, in all the ways that matter. What ways are those?–I asked. You know, like family,

Megan said. Dog nosed at the trailer door to go outside. He's an outsidedog, but he loves Megan enough to sleep indoors now. She's been trying to give him a better name than Dog. Duke, she called him, King, Royalty. He won't answer to anything but Dog. He is what he is, I told her. I want him to feel good about himself, Megan said, rubbing the soft spot between his eyes. I asked her about the church's singing, about how it gets closer at night. Do they know about me?–I asked. They've heard some rumors about you, Megan said, from people passing through. I let Dog out and watched him roam off into the desert. Then, he went further than my eyes could see. It makes Megan nervous when he disappears like that, but I don't worry. Dog knows what he's doing. Dog will outlive us all. You ought to stop going there, I told her. I can't, she said. They all knew my mother and my brother. Megan's brother's name was Gavin and she tells me about him in postage-stamp-sized increments. He loved Pixie Stix and Mountain Dew. Anything with too much sugar in it. He loved video games because they made him feel important, like the hero of something, although he wouldn't say that's what he liked. He'd say he liked the violence or the exaggerated boobs. He was a sweet boy who grew up twisted, Megan said. Like a tree trunk strangled by a vine. He had blonde hair and when he hung himself, his skin turned purple. Yellow and purple are complementary colors, Megan said, and I nodded. I flipped over my tarot cards while she talked about her brother so that I had something to look at other than her face. It makes her feel safe if my eyes are pointed elsewhere. It's not like he was special, Megan said. He was like a million other people. But, I don't know, his feet swinging like that. You're right, I told her. He didn't deserve that despair. Where does Dog go when he runs out into the desert?–Megan asked, and I shrugged, palmed the cards in front of me on the kitchen table. It doesn't surprise me that you found the red tent in the woods, although I'm sure it shocked *you* a little. It doesn't surprise me that you dragged it all from the earth with your hands. You want to know everything. But, once you know, what can you do? The investments have been made. I remember my mother's body being laid gentle into the earth. Hearing her sigh in my mind like she'd just put her feet into a tub of hot water. She got out just in time. Then Megan asked me the question she always asks. Do you think it looks like rain?

It was easy to not talk about the red tent in the woods. I had to make my baby food, I had to make sure my nephews didn't start fighting, I had to keep my sister and her husband from switching radio stations every ten seconds. It's not the truth, my brother-in-law said, switching to his preferred station, one that broadcast the news from the underground, whose frequency sounded like whale songs, who said it was worse, so much worse, than we thought. Fuck your truth, my sister whispered so that the boys couldn't hear. She turned back her radio to a station that was rebuilding itself. Anchors whose voices we knew. It was getting better, my sister's radio said. All we needed was patience. How can we know if we never leave the mountain? Between all this, my father snuck out to the garage to pull bong hits. I snuck out with him for the first time since I was nineteen. Weed's gotten stronger. Remember how cool I thought I was in high school? That beautiful boy by the lake? I wonder what happened to him. Remember how badly you wanted to get drunk with us. You know, I don't think about any of the other boys, but I still think about him, blonde in the darkness, sixteen. I guess the first gets branded onto you somehow. You were mad for like a week and then I could see it dawning in your eyes that teenage romance never lasts. You just had to wait him out. My father hands me his silicone bong. Strong stuff, he warns me. When I was a kid, he would sneak down to the basement to smoke and he'd tell us that he was folding laundry, which I knew he never did. Remember when my hamster died and he found all the Mike's Hard Lemonade in my sister's closet because he was looking for a shoebox, a hamster coffin? They screamed at each other at the top of the stairs while I held my hamster and cried. That hamster got buried in the Mike's Hard Lemonade box. You laughed and laughed and then made me a widow's veil out of your mother's old fishnet stockings. I take an enormous bong hit and the hard edges of the world smooth themselves out a bit. Smoke and that smell, like grass, but acidic. I cough and my dad laughs at me. He says, it's been a minute? And I say, yeah, since college. Since that first year after you took off and I suddenly didn't have a best friend and there was a part of me that liked that. I thought I could be someone new, but that meant someone worse, someone less than who I'd been when you were there. I was high a lot during my first year of college. I saw the posters that hung on the boys' walls. How they said I was pretty, but in a girl-pretty way. There's girl-pretty and boy-pretty, they said. Like, the kind of pretty that sells perfume and expensive ugly clothes and the kind of pretty that sells cars and boats. I never thought I was pretty, never. Not even when the blonde boy's eyes went soft by the bonfire and he touched my face with the tips of his fingers. Not even when my husband said, Hey, Beautiful. He called me that, still calls me it. No, not until I saw myself reflected in my baby, did I think, *perfect,* did I think, *just right.* And now I have these stretch marks, but I love them because they're proof she grew inside me. My dad is talking, but I can't listen to what he's saying and I like floating above the concrete floor of this garage, but even though I'm shrouded in smoke and I can faintly hear my sister and brother-in-law toggle between doom and a cheerful façade, I still see the red tent from the corner of my eyes. I still see it flashing, underneath leaves and dirt, like someone had something to hide.

MEGAN LIKES THE BEER TOO MUCH. SHE CAME back from church with a handle of vodka swinging at her side. Where'd you get that?–I asked, and she said none of your business, and I said give me some. So, me and Megan and Dog walked out to the desert and watched it get dark and passed the bottle between us. Dog sniffed the bottle's wet mouth and shied away from the harshness inside it. Dogs are smart, Megan said, her voice slurring. She's a lightweight. She weighs nothing. I laugh, grab some more, look up at the sky. In the moments between day and night the horizon is lit up with fire. We heard about the fires in the city. A pilgrim told us that everything plastic melted into abstract shapes that looked like screaming faces. After the pilgrim left, Megan said, Now there's nowhere to go. No, seriously, where'd you get the booze? From the pastor, Megan said, laughing. She wiped her lips with the back of her bony wrist and I thought of her mother, the circles under her mother's eyes. I thought of her shoddy funeral. The thump of her shrouded body hitting the red dirt. The women did the digging. The pastor stood apart, flames in his eyes, he was something else. He's the one who gave Megan's mother the pills. Who's his connection?—I asked. Where could he get the pills? No one comes here anymore. Except to see you, Megan said, which made me think of the silence of an open grave. I guess God is his connection, Megan said, and then she clapped her hand over her mouth, outraged at her own blasphemy—but I liked the beer, she said, so I asked if he had any and he said no but he did have this vodka and he said that we all need something sometimes to get us through things. Get us through what?—I asked. Things, Megan said, swirling her fingers in the sky as if to say, all of this, Existence, so okay, fine, then, don't gift a horse mouth in the . . . look . . . or whatever. . . . And I couldn't help it, I laughed. She's like a child when she's drunk, gangly and disarming. I wonder what her pastor would have said if I'd taken her into my bed. I think your pastor has flames in his eyes, I told her, and she shook her hair in front of her face, blew it up in the air with a puff from her lips. Dog yelped. The desert grew dark. I swear, I could feel a little tingling, like I was getting drunk. Maybe the tips of my toes were getting drunk. You ever been with a man?–Megan asked. Once. On the road. I took his motorcycle jacket. You love him? A little. We met in a bar and he was a hard thing to knock my body against. I liked the pain then. I like pain, Megan said. Don't be so maudlin. I do!–Megan pinched the white flesh of her inner arm until it turned bright red. Stop that. She kept pinching. When I drink it's harder to feel but I still like it. It's the numb you've got to watch out for. When Mom died I was all numb for two whole days. I didn't like that speech the pastor gave at her funeral. He'd stood at the lip of Megan's mother's grave and said she was at peace now. That she'd gone to the Lord. He made it sound good, dying. He made it sound like a vacation. He talks to God, Megan said. He knows. He knows what's up. You don't believe that. Sure I do. I believe in you and I believe in him. I'm hedging my bets. I could see the flesh above Megan's armpit begin to bruise. It made me think of those piles of melted plastic. I remember how cool I thought you were in high school, when you were drunk or high. How above it all. When I took off on that motorcycle I tried getting drunk or high, stronger stuff than in high school. None of it ever worked. I never transcended my existence. Not even for a second. Listen, I said to Megan, maybe stop going to church for a while. Or, like, skip tomorrow at least. I'm afraid they'll fuck you up if you go every day. *Pshhhh,* Megan said, like water coming out of a hose. *Pssssh.* You're not my mother.

Out in the garage, I feel underwater. Under smoke. Marijuana.
I never liked being high. The first time in college I made the
boys lock all the windows. Convinced someone was coming
for me. Later, I lay on a bed and didn't care much what
happened to me. That's the thing. Marijuana. I don't much
care, so I just walk back into the kitchen, eyes red, red eyes.
My baby is asleep. My baby is asleep or I would never be
high; I want you to know that, although I'm also thinking
maybe I'll be high forever now, which is what I always think
whenever my consciousness is altered, I think, *so this is how it'll
always be,* but anyway, I'm not afraid now that I'm cloaked in
smoke. I smell good, like a bonfire, plus weed. Weed smells
good. Mom, I say, once I make it to the kitchen. Outside,
it's dark; we couldn't see a herd of deer walk past the kitchen
window if they walked past now. They'd be invisible. Mom,
I say again, and she looks over at me. What? What did you
do to that man?–I ask, that man with the tent that I found
under leaves. You did something. What was it? My mother
shakes her head. You're smoking with your father? You know
his tolerance is higher than yours. I know, but I no longer
care. I am unreachable in my marijuana cloud. Everything

is murky. Everything is clear. You hurt him or scared him off or what? My mother's eyes don't look confused, they look hard. Whatever was done is done, my sister says. Whatever was done?—I ask, what was it? What was done? But, no one will tell me. If you don't tell me I'll go out into those woods. I'll find his body or whatever. Did you kill him? I'll bring his skeleton back here. Did you know that early Anglo-Saxons, pre-Romans stuffed the bodies of their dead and hung their preserved corpses from the eaves of their homes? Over the hearth. Eyeballs cut out, they watched. Calm down, my mother says. It's okay, says my sister. My husband is in our bedroom singing a song to my sleeping baby and I feel the pull at the center of my torso, the pull toward her, and I know that I'm talking nonsense. I know I won't go out into the woods now to find the corpse of the outsideman. Because that's what I'm certain is out there under the leaves. His body. His bones. How? Who? Someone must have killed him. Snuck up in the night. A memory of my mother and sister whispering in the hallway. It's not like there are laws anymore, my brother-in-law says, but my sister shakes her head at him in a sharp moment so he doesn't keep talking. It's not like there are laws. Who would I report my family to, even if I could report them? I look at my father, spaced-out, eyes red; tell me it's okay, I say to him. Tell me nothing happened. What are you talking about, sweetheart?—he asks, touching down briefly onto this plane of existence. You shouldn't worry about it, my sister says, it's over. So, I sit on the sofa and stare at nothingness. I feel my body like it's underwater. I see my reflection in the glass door. Beyond it is the woods, down the mountain to the fire, overtop of so many bones.

IF YOU COULD HEAR ME, I'D TELL YOU WHAT
happened to your outsideman. I could feel it in the night. A lot
of death in the desert. The church never seems to dwindle,
though. New people, long sleeves, come every day. The last of
the ragtags, the junkies, and the petty criminals, hightailing
it. It looks like the desert is being reclaimed for the Lord.
I tell Megan not to go, but she laughs and asks me what
should she do with her time instead? Stay in the trailer with
me and Dog? And I say, why not? What's wrong with that?
I flip my cards over, trying to see what's going to come of all
their singing, all their passion, but I know. I know before
the woman in the long-sleeved ankle-length dress comes to
the door. She's so covered up it's ostentatious. Like I'd look.
She has a pamphlet. She's heard about me. Megan talks
about you, she says, and I see Megan's eyes go wide. I've
got a card in my hands, one of my favorite cards, The Fool.
Thanks, I say, taking her pamphlet. You should come pray
with us sometime, she says. Pray for what? Pray for rain. And
I think, how human, to sit in the desert and pray for rain
instead of moving. How human to be certain that rain will
come. What's the new date?–I ask. I'm sorry? The new date
after which you'll kill yourselves if it stays dry? The woman's
cheeks redden and I think maybe their suicidal ideation is
supposed to be a secret. Maybe I've gotten Megan in trouble
now. I don't know what you mean, the woman says, so I shrug

and pretend to read the pamphlet. I ask her if she wants her future told. I feel her hesitate in front of me. She does. I can feel it, tendrils of want. Remember when I read your high school boyfriend's future and he was disappointed because he was destined for nothing great or unusual? And I said he was lucky and he said what was the point of living if you were going to be living like everyone else? I wonder where he is now, if he's still a handsome blonde boy under his years. No thank you, the woman says. I look into her face. There are lines there, loss. Loss like everyone else's loss, spiky like cactus spines. Say, listen, I'll tell you something for free. She doesn't tell me to go ahead, but she doesn't tell me to stop either. That preacher is going to be the death of you, I say. The woman pulls her mouth together like a drawstring bag. She hates what I've said, but she's heard it. She turns and walks away without saying another word, and I watch the dust she kicks up with her feet. Megan, still drunk, laughs hysterically once she's gone. Man, I thought I was going to pass out watching her, Megan says. She holds herself way too tight. I nod and Megan hiccups and I think about all the vodka I drank and how I still can't feel a thing. Megan's shit-faced, but when she's quiet, it's hard to tell. Why'd you tell them about me?–I ask. They asked, Megan says, like it's natural. Like it's a friendly curiosity. You shouldn't have told her that thing about the preacher though, Megan says, as I shuffle The Fool back into the deck. She's going to tell him what you said. Yeah, well, I say to my deck of cards, we'll see, I say to the pictures under my hands as I reach into them and turn over another card.

Even now, when I dream an anxious dream, it makes me think of you. In the dream my body is younger and I hate it like I did when I was a teen girl. I hated my body for so long and then when I had my daughter, it did a little stutter-step—ta-da!—and I felt bad for never realizing what my body could do. That its primary function was never ornamental. It keeps life alive, is what I mean. I'm young and I hate my body, but I'm prettier than I'll ever be again and my high school boyfriend knows it. He's got green eyes like the boys in romance books, green eyes and blond hair and he's so ordinary, but to me he's a knife blade or something to cut myself on. And I'm in the backseat of his car, in this anxiety dream, and he's on top of me, kissing me, pushing my young hated body into the metal of the seatbelt and it's hot and it's awkward and then there's a knock on the door. A knock on the car door from the outside. My high school boyfriend shifts his hips and opens the door and his raw mouth says, What? And it's me. It's older me. Stretch-marks, less beautiful, but grander in scale. The full height of my powers, such as they are. Future me is mouthing something to teenage me, still stuck under the blonde boy and I squint and I peer but I can't make out what I'm saying. My boyfriend rolls his eyes and shuts the door and keeps kissing me, but I can't focus on the kissing anymore. All I can think about is my face, my older face full of gravitas and emotion and what it was trying to tell me. That's the anxiety dream I have after I pass out, high, convinced that my mother had the outsideman killed. I can't imagine her—pearl necklace—doing the killing with her own hands. There was no blood. Maybe poison? Poison with what? Who did the violence? Who hurt his body? I left my high school boyfriend after you disappeared, disgusted with everything that had attracted me—the tight coil of muscles in his back, his wide-open face like a windowpane in the sun. He cried, asked me why I didn't want him, and I told him to get over it. We were young. It was just a minute. One minute of time. My heart is still thumping in the dark bedroom, my husband asleep beside me, curled on his side like a fetus in a womb, he's big and grown and much better than my high school boyfriend. I can't think of what I'm trying to tell myself. Was it a warning? Was it telling me to enjoy the world while I could before everything became THE CATASTROPHE? I remember kissing in my high school boyfriend's car, the week before your father kicked you out and I never saw you again. I remember that moment so clearly it haunts me, though at the time I thought of nothing but his young body on top of me, obliterating me with his weight. I used to think I didn't have it in me to hurt anybody.

IT'S FUNNY THAT YOU DREAM OF HIGH SCHOOL when you dream. I almost never do. High school is in my head while I'm awake—you're still in my head. I haven't lost you the way you've lost me. When I have to dream about fear, I dream about the girl with the multi-colored markers, the one who's sending pilgrims to me even now. I dream about her gray eyes, cold, even though I'm sure in life that her eyes were brown. I dream about the dead whale. That's you, she said. And I said, What? What do you mean? And she drew a dead whale on the thin skin of my wrist with a red marker. Little crabs come to eat you, she said. Sometimes I wake up sweating, hearing her high lilting voice saying little crabs come to eat you. I loved her when I shouldn't have. I don't blame you for kissing your high school boyfriend in the car. I kissed a man in the back of a bar while the sticky clack of pool balls sounded over the jukebox. I stole his leather jacket. The arms were long, they covered up all my scars. He said, It's not glamorous to be damaged, he said it like he knew. I told him I wasn't trying to be glamorous. I told him that if I was going to be a witch, I was going to be the gray-haired gravel-voiced kind, like my mother. I wasn't going to seduce men to steal their things. I cured his bad dreams before I left him, a pulse of light to his temple. I rode my motorcycle to the beach straight after, made a bee-line for a little woman in a long skirt carrying multi-colored markers in her hands. She drew a turtle on my ankle the first day we met and said tortoises are patient and I told her that she'd drawn a sea turtle and she frowned and said that sea turtles were buoyant, but were mostly plastic these days. I said I was a witch and she said cool. I never tried to cure whatever was wrong in her head. I was afraid to touch it. To invite it in. I dream about her, not about you, not about the man whose leather jacket I wear, whenever it feels like the night is circling me. Dog barks if I wake up, startled, in the night. Megan, still curled on the futon, shifts and mumbles, but doesn't wake. I stare at my dark ceiling and think of you atop your lonely mountain, so sure that violence has occurred outside, but unable to prove it. I wish I could close my eyes and be next to you. Next to your strong husband curled up like a shrimp in your bed. I wish I could pick up your blonde baby and kiss a blessing onto her nose. In the cool air I'd soothe your dreams, but unstopper the mouth of your vision. It's a warning. You know that. It's a warning and you never listen. If I stay still enough in my bed and listen with all my might, I can hear the church singing on the desert air.

I spend the morning in my bedroom, staring at the ceiling, avoiding my mother. My husband wakes the baby who stretches her arms around his neck. I still feel the pull towards her, but it's weaker because I'm afraid. I'm afraid of the living room. Afraid of my family's faces. It's not until almost lunchtime that I get up because I hear my sister scream. She's screaming at the top of her lungs like she used to when my parents found liquor in her closet growing up. Roaring at the teenaged injustice. Not being able to control your own destiny. Roaring. I get up, pad to the living room. My sister is running towards the woods. My nephews were playing hide and seek. They can't find my red-haired nephew. They think he went outside. My sister runs to the trees. My mother stands in the doorway and watches. What if he's just hiding in here?—I ask, but my mother doesn't seem to hear me. She worries her pearls in her fingers. I'll go, I tell my husband, I say to the face of my baby, I'll go to the woods, you stay here. It feels good to leave the house. The air feels fresh. I'm shouting my sister's name. She's shouting for her son. When I

96

catch up to her she's hysterical, her face red and wet. He can't have gone far, I tell her. He can't have gone far. We walk the circular path and call his name. The trees echo back to us. It's still daylight, I say. It's daylight and he might be in the house anyway. He might be under the bed. My sister doesn't say anything. She's grave and the pull inside of her, that mother pull, tells her that her boy went to the woods. We follow it. Tugging. We follow it deeper and around. I wonder what we'll do if he went off the path. Then, ahead, a blue t-shirt, red hair. My sister screams. She breaks into a run. My nephew turns and looks at his mother, flying down upon him like a bird of prey, her arms thrown out wide. Behind my nephew stands the outsideman. He backs away, puts his hands up in the air. My sister punches him in the face, grabs her boy and starts running back to the house. She's a blur. She's a wildcat's scream. I am frozen. I watch the outsideman stagger and clutch his nose. I watch the blood pool between his fingers. I thought they killed you, I say and he nods. He understands. They just chased me away, he says, behind bubbles of blood. I can't think of anything else other than to take my shirt off and offer it to him. I'm wearing a sports bra. He can see the stretch marks on my belly where I grew my daughter. He presses my shirt to his face and nods his thanks. I didn't take the boy, he says. I didn't take him; I was just out here and I saw him walking; he walked up to me. The outsideman takes a step towards me, his hands palm-up in supplication. I'm shivering. Afraid. I turn and run back the way my sister ran. I feel foolish for giving the outsideman my shirt and then foolish for thinking my mother and sister killed him. What'd I think? That they'd smothered him in the night? That they'd dragged his body into the underbrush? Yes, I thought that.

Back at the cabin, my sister is on her knees in front of her red-haired boy. Don't you ever go wandering like that, she's saying, close, closer to his face. I just wanted to see the man, the boy whimpers, I just wanted to see if he's alright. The family turns to see me in the doorway, shirtless in my sports bra. I gave him . . . for his nose, I say. They turn their heads from me. My husband brings my baby to my face. You can't go wandering, my sister says to her boy. My husband kisses the top of my head. My baby reaches her arms out for me. You don't know what's out there, my sister says.

THREE

"Why, if it was an illusion, not praise the catastrophe, whatever it was, that destroyed illusion and put truth in its place?"

—Virginia Woolf, *A Room of One's Ow*

THE CHURCH PEOPLE COME CLOSER IN THE morning. I'm out taking a piss under the stars when I see them moving as a group towards my trailer. I will Megan to wake up. You should've known that your mother and sister didn't kill a man. I bet you didn't think you were capable of thinking it. Capable of thinking it and of deciding to let it go. The church people come closer. I move back towards the trailer, my long t-shirt blowing in the wind, I hear the girl with the multi-colored markers say little crabs come to eat you. They're singing, the church people. They're singing under the lightening sky as if their voices bring the sunrise. I want to shout that they've got nothing to do with it, that it's timing—that's all. I see the woman from before, the one I told to watch out for the preacher, that he'd be the death of them. I see him. He stands out in a crowd. Pressed white. Clean. Manic behind the eyes. He's on fire with himself.

On fire with the idea of himself on fire. Megan comes out of the trailer. I hear Dog snuffle the air, catching the scent of so many bodies so close. There must be two dozen church people plus their preacher, singing to the sky. I can't make out the words they're singing, or even if they're singing words at all. The preacher man is shouting, but he's drowned out under their voices, rising, falling, chirping, calling, they're beautiful on the wind. Megan and Dog come to stand beside me. There's nothing to do but stand and watch them. When they get close enough that I can tell their faces apart, they stop. The preacher man lifts his arms. He's got a book. He's shouting at me, but there's a roar in my ears like the ocean, like the crash and swirl of my own blood magnified back in the soul of a shell. He's shouting something about God and Rain, but all I hear is the clack of pool balls in a bar. All I can see is their song. Megan puts her hand on my forearm, as if to restrain me. As if, whatever the preacher man is saying, it would make me mad enough to charge. But I don't hear him, I hear Megan's brother dangling from a rope. I hear the thud of Megan's mother's body hitting the ground. I hear a shovel shoveling earth. I hear a can of food, tinted windows, fires, breaking glass, helicopter, then nothing, then the howl of the wind, then nothing, then rain. I lift my palm up to the air to see if it's going to rain, but no, it's a memory. A powerful memory. I'm on my motorcycle, the one I stole, driving away from my father's red face screaming, and I'm crying because I'll miss you and I'll miss my mother and the girl I used to be and then it's raining and I'm riding in the rain and I am the rain and we're falling together. I smile at that memory at the comfort of it. And then I hear the silence and I know the preacher man has stopped preaching. He wants me to respond.

101

I feel guilty for thinking that my family killed a man. But, if you take a man's tent and chase him into the woods—isn't that killing him, kind of? I read my baby a book on the sofa and try to avoid looking over at them. My sister hasn't calmed down, even though her son is back in the house and safe and fine. He wandered out on his own. The outsideman had nothing to do with it, he says, in his small boy voice. He says that he was walking the path like we've done a hundred times before. Running into the outsideman was a coincidence, he says. We didn't chase him far enough, my sister says. We should have chased him all the way down the mountain. The book I'm reading to my baby features a blue whale. I wonder if there are still whales? I've been thinking about them lately—I don't know why. Their huge bodies casting shadows in the sea. Their eerie songs. Since the tiniest things, insects and crawling things, buzzing things, algae, bacteria, amoebas and things are gone, plastic, something destroyed them, does that mean there's no charismatic megafauna left? SAVE THE ALGAE bumper sticker. You, who could actually save things, got run out of town. I remember your mother's empty pill bottle, how she was almost dead, how you put your hands on her and she rose, but you fell. How your father screamed and screamed that you were playing God. Like he wanted your mother to die. Maybe he did? Maybe you ruined his plans? Do you remember how we had to sit in the woods? How I held your head in my lap while you recovered. Because your mother was almost dead, you were almost dead for a while. Pale. A pale flicker of who you were. And you said, tell me a story. Above our heads, the trees of the cul-de-sac nodded. I told you a story of a praying mantis, but it was too violent. Tell me a nice story you said, so I told you about people who live underground and they're happy and nothing bad happens to them. I wonder, if your mother was all the way dead, if you could have brought her back with your life. If your lips would have turned all the way blue. I got up when you felt better and said don't move. I said I'd be right back. I don't understand why you went back to your house, palms reaching for your mother. Why you ran when you ran, why you didn't wait for me. I should have tracked you down. I wonder if the outsideman will come back? My baby points at the blue whale spouting water in her book. It makes me think of the blue of your mother's lips. How she wanted to die then. How she did die later. Whale, I say to my baby, whose eyes are blue like water. She nods, grave, as if she understands that there were once many blue things that no longer are.

I RAISE MY HANDS AND WAVE AT THE CHURCH
people. Hello, I say, smiling a little. Megan looks at me,
horrified. Is hello not what I was supposed to say? It's funny
that you're thinking of my mother's blue lips, her body
akimbo on the bedspread, my hands warming her back up,
the weakness that fell upon me, my father's rage. My father
is not unlike this preacher, although I guess there's a good
chance that he's dead now too. Dead with our cul-de-sac
overrun with vines. Maybe he's akimbo on the marital bed.
Bones. Those vines are an invasive species. Remember that
neighbor lady with the yellow crocs who tried to get everyone
to agree to pull them out? Where does a lady like that get off
telling a vine it's invasive? You have to say something, Megan
says. What? I ask. Show that you mean no harm. She whispers
out of the side of her mouth like we used to when we snuck
underneath the branches of trees by the lake. Your blonde
boy never learned how to whisper. He hooted like a cartoon
owl. That moonlit night. Water droplets like crystals before
everything got too hot. Hoot hoot, your blonde boy said, and
I rolled my eyes. What do you see in him? But I knew, you
saw his body, his mouth, the solid weight of his confidence.
I don't mean you any harm, I say to the preacher man and
his church people. They look like they don't believe me. The
woman who came before shouts at me about telling the future.
About how it's a sin. I tell her the future is written, isn't it?
Isn't that what they believe? Nothing I say will change the
writing on the wall. There's a nodding, a murmuring. And
anyway, I say, most people who come to see me know the
answers to their questions. They just want me to say it so
they don't have to. More murmurs, more nods. More than

one church person has knocked on my trailer door asking a question they knew the answer to. Love and sex and money. Change and death and rebirth. The preacher man might feel that he's losing his audience so he makes a show of raising their holy book above his head. I'm inviting you to church, he says. I'm inviting you to call down the rain. You think we're gonna call down the rain? It's going to rain, he says, with all the confidence of the blonde boy at night, pretending to be an owl. Well, okay, I say because it's hot and I don't want to stand outside anymore. I realize that I'm the last odd thing left in the carcass of this town. That without me, the church people would have nothing to talk about. It's a comforting thought. I serve my purpose. They wouldn't want to eliminate me, right? But then, my father's face, unbidden, red and veiny, shouting as my mother lifted her heavy head. What have you done? Are you the devil? Shouting, angry, when I thought he'd be pleased that I saved her. There are so many things I don't understand about that moment, but I know why I ran. Why I didn't wait for you. I thought that what my father said was true. That I was bad, evil, and I didn't want to hurt you. I didn't want to drag you down with me. Say you'll go to church, Megan whispers and I prevent myself from rolling my eyes. Okay, I say. Sure, why not? The church people seem happy. In all their modest clothing, they sweat, they turn around. It's time to retreat from the sun. The preacher watches the longest but he, too, eventually turns. We go back inside the trailer. Megan bites the inside of her cheek. It makes her look worried, I hope she doesn't draw blood. My mother almost killed herself once, I tell Megan. She looks up at me like she knew all about it. But, I say, I put my hands on her and brought her back.

In bed, hush, quiet, everything gray, quiet. When the dogs bark I am so awake, the blood rushes to my head. I leap out of bed, like, what? Like I'm going to hit whatever is making the dogs bark with my fist. My husband rubs his face. I'll check, I say and he nods, settles back in. The house is quiet. Maybe I'm the only one who heard the dogs bark? The cat twines her body around my ankles as I move through the kitchen, looking for a treat. I think of my baby in her crib. How she didn't even stir. The dogs are at the door, looking out. I turn on the porch light and there he is. Of course he is. The outsideman returns. I open the door a crack. He looks at me, frowns, sheepish, as if he wishes he had somewhere else to be. What are you doing here?–I ask. His nose is bruised, his eyes puffy. I went down the mountain and there's nothing there, he says. Please, he says to me. Wait here, I say. I lock the door and leave the light on. He stands on the porch, leaning like a willow sapling. I grab slices of bread, make a PB&J, mom muscle memory. I bring him the sandwich and the bottle of water. He looks so grateful I might cry. You know you can't stay here, I say. You know they'll hurt you. But you won't hurt me?–the outsideman asks. He looks at me with eyes, blue like my daughter's, full of something and I can't tell, I can never tell friend from foe. I won't, I say. He nods. Let me sleep under the porch, he says. Don't tell them. Just tonight, I whisper. Just for tonight. He nods, wipes his mouth. They took my tent, he says. They shoved me and yelled at me and took my tent. I know, I say. I rub my face with my hands. So tired. So tired. I don't know this man. What if my sister's right? What if he's got something bloody planned? Maybe he senses the shift in my thoughts because he gets up and thanks me again. I watch him hop down off of the porch, he folds himself underneath it like a shadow. Ship in a bottle. Tiny sails. I turn off the porch light and wait for a long time, my face close to the glass in the dark. I wait, but everything stays dark and still. It makes me think of your mother's room when she had migraines, or of the woods where we ran after I had careless sex with that blonde boy, and I cried and clutched my stomach and asked you what I was going to do. You touched my stomach and I got my period the next day and it was early but I'm still not sure if you did anything or not. You who could call on blood to appear. I wish your face would appear in the dark. You, with your light in your hands. I wish you would roll up on your motorcycle and pull this outsideman, this moral conundrum, out from under the porch and take him away. I bet you know a place that's still living. I bet you could find him somewhere to live. I don't hear my husband's footsteps approaching, but he's gentle, he puts his arms around my waist, kisses my neck. Is all sleepy murmurs. What is it?—he asks and I tell him about the outsideman because we have no secrets. Just for tonight?—he asks. That's what I said, I whisper, but now I'm afraid to leave the doorway. I'm afraid he'll set the cabin on fire. I'll stay up, my husband says. I'll stay up and watch. We'll stay up together. And we do. We sit on the sofa, our limbs entwined in darkness and watch the porch and wait to see if anything will make a move.

SITTING IN THE TRAILER AFTER THE CHURCH
people have gone, Megan is giving me a funny look. What?–I
ask. Something just occurred to me, she says. Well? The girl
who drew on you with colored markers is pointing people
this way. She's sending people to you. Right. Well, how does
she know you're here? How does she know enough to draw a
map to this spot? I laugh. It huffs out of me like one of Dog's
sighs. Oh, that, I say. Well? Well, she knows I'm here. She
followed me when I tried to flee. She said that I belonged by
the sea. With her? I belonged by the water, water called to
me, all that sort of thing. Does it? Megan asks. Sometimes, I
say. Sometimes water and sometimes trees. Anything growing
can call to me. I hear things in the lives of plants, animals,
algae floating on the sea's smooth surface. So you came to the
desert? I came when everything started to die off. The little
voices. The bees. Remember bees? Megan scrunches up her
nose and tries to remember a bee. Fat and fuzzy, bumbling
from flowerhead to flowerhead. I used to hear their voices
like a song, I say. That sounds nice. Well, the girl with the
multi-colored markers mostly leaves me alone now. She tried
to seduce me back to living places, but I never followed her.
I told her I wanted quiet. I told her I was done with her and
done with answering people's questions. So she sends people

to you? It's very like her to do that, I say. I collapse back on my bed and Megan curls up on the futon with Dog. We could stay like this in the trailer forever, as far as I'm concerned. You saved Giles, Megan whispers. Yeah, I say, but I don't have enough in me to save a whole lot more than that. Dog whines with pleasure as Megan scratches behind his ears. You're seriously going to go to the church to call down the rain? It doesn't seem like I have a choice, I say. I think you should, she says. I think if anybody can make it rain, it's you. Nobody can make it rain now, I say. Maybe twenty years ago we all could have made it rain if we tried hard enough, but now. . . . It'll give people hope, Megan says. We close our eyes. We're ready to nap through the rest of the day's heat. Later, I'll have to unearth some more nonperishables from their hiding spot. Megan is eating me out of my stores. But it's worth it, for the company. If I have to, I can pull the sandy tarp off of my motorcycle and ride somewhere to steal cans. I wonder if that's why your outsideman came back. Because the mountain and the broken town are empty and he doesn't even have a dog. He's alone. He's lonely. Maybe he just wanted to see another human face. You saved Giles, Megan murmurs as she's drifting off to sleep. The gecko is in his terrarium cursed by my hands to a long life of confinement.

We wake with the dogs sleeping at our feet. There is sun on the porch. My eyes open first, I'm gripped with fear. What if we fell asleep and he crawled in through the window and ate the baby? What if it was all a dream? I shake my husband's shoulder, he wakes. We stare. He, being the husband, gets up and opens the door. I watch him with the dogs, their wet noses pressed to the glass. They whine like they whine when we grill meat. I watch my husband bend and look under the porch. We all cease to exist for a moment. He straightens, looks at me, shakes his head. Back inside, he says there's no one there. Just a soft impression in the dirt where the outsideman, or an animal, curled. We go back into our bedroom and look at our baby, asleep in her crib. She has slept through all of this uncertainty. I remember when your mother died, this time for real. I remember the funeral, pre-CATASTROPHE, but post-you leaving my life. I was home from college on autumn break, wearing an orange sweater over my black dress, standing with my family at her open gravesite. Listening as the catholic priest intoned something about ashes, how we're from ashes, ashes, how we return to ashes. The cliche distracting me from the truth. I flicked my eyes over the treeline, but you weren't there, leaning, smoking a cigarette, wearing a leather jacket, like you would have been if it was a movie. Your mother died of heart failure, your father said.

Heart failure. I think of her coffin being lowered as I turn my back on the outsideman. I hope he's gone for good. I feel bad for hoping. When THE CATASTROPHE started, I remember my mother saying it won't be bad, it won't get worse, it won't affect you. Everyone I knew reacted first with confusion. We'd read about things like this, creeping over the horizon. But, my husband, in the homeless shelter in the city, saw the waves and waves of desperation crown, crash, recede, crown, over all of our heads. He was the first one to say pack a bag, put your ID in it. People said let's go to Canada, as if Canada could maintain a border if we fell apart. Drones. Guns guns guns. We went to the mountains as the fires burned. Where was the outsideman when all of this started? Was he inside? Was he a drug counselor? Did he lead a local bird-watching group? Or, more likely, was he curled like a shrimp under a concrete bridge, sitting in the drip-drip of our runoff, dreaming of my uncle's illicit cabin? Something I wish he would have told me before he disappeared: how did he know my uncle? My husband puts his arms around my waist and we lean together, looking down at our sleeping baby. You think he'll be back?—my husband murmurs into the skin of my neck. Crown, crash, recede, crown. Maybe, I whisper, as above our heads the rest of the house comes to life. There's a gun in the garage, my husband says.

THE MASS OF THE RAIN IS JUST AS INSANE AS it sounds. I'm with Megan. I've dug out my old leather jacket just for the occasion. No, I didn't wear it to my mother's funeral. I didn't want to risk meeting my father's eyes over a sweltering plate of deli meats. I rode my motorcycle back and put my hand on her name carved in stone. Night. Rain. I cried alone. I'd read about her death online. My father used a picture from before her hair went white. The preacher man is on a round stage in the middle of us. The church used to be a bar, but there's no more liquor. Liquor ran out months ago here. I bet, in the city, behind swaying topiaries, there's plenty of liquor. Liquor gushing out of Cupid's puckered mouth. I smile. The preacher man frowns at me, so I keep smiling, imagining all the weird things rich people get up to behind their hedges. The mass of the rain is severe, and not, in fact, a mass—that's just a catholic thing. It's a harangue. From what I can tell it hasn't rained because we're all miserable sinners. The preacher man paces back and forth on top of the old bar, where drunk girls no doubt used to flash patrons. Where belly shots were no doubt sucked down. He says that God is withholding water, withholding one essential element of life—he says life like he's saying knife—because of our miserable sinfulness. The crowd around me looks dazed. They seem used to his shouts and recriminations. It makes me wonder about all of their fathers. How many get screamed at like I got screamed at, but mistook that fear for love? Megan is absently sucking on the end of one stringy braid. They seem to know this badness in their hearts. They are well-acquainted with the rottenness inside of their souls. It makes me think of my girl with the multi-colored markers. You're like that. The dead whale. The last time she came to see me, to try to convince me to come back to the ocean, her eyes flashed like a storm on the horizon and she said I'd never be complete because there was a piece of me, a nick, that fell out a long time ago. Too small to ever be found. Too sharp to fix. I rolled my eyes, but it hurt me. Stung like a bee sting of truth. I watched her go and thought about moving again. Thought about digging myself a hole where she'd never find me. She'd left one last drawing on my forearm. A ship rocked on the seas of a vicious storm. COWARD it said on its triangle sail. Drawn in orange. It took weeks to fade. I'm not listening to the preacher man, obviously. I'm waiting to see if he'll slip in his shiny shoes and tumble off the bar. Waiting to see if he'll crack his skull on something and free these people from his eyes. Then, everyone turns. They start walking. What? I ask Megan and she smiles at me because she knows I haven't been paying attention. Outside, the old neon lights are busted. Nothing glows. The stars are obscene. We feel ourselves spin. The preacher man is marching us somewhere. Where? I ask. Around me, people have their eyes on their feet, damn the universe's starry display. To the desert, Megan whispers. She's smiling wider now, giddy. He's going to make us shout at the sky. I laugh. I look up. The stars wink down at me. At this childish temper tantrum. They regard us with good humor, I think. Change, death, rebirth, change, death. The tricky part is knowing which.

There's a gun in the garage and it glows in my mind. Danger, danger, danger. Like a revolving neon sign. Like the ones that used to say Girls Girls Girls. Don't they know what happens once you introduce a gun? Don't they know what inevitably comes from its shadow on the wall? My mother bought the gun on our way out of town, my husband says. She bought it in exchange for some gold rings out of the back of a red Ford F-150. She doesn't know how to use it. She hasn't told anyone about it, except for the men. The men all know because men are supposed to know about guns, but out of all of us, I think, the men are the least likely to pull the trigger. Does it have bullets?—I ask, and my husband nods. It has enough to kill us all twice over. My mother bought it because she thought THE CATASTROPHE might be the end of things and sometimes you need a quicker way to the end. Don't tell your sister, my husband says. I won't because I don't want to live through the scene when she finds out. There are children in this house!—She'll scream. Pre-catastrophe, anyway that's what she'd scream. Now, maybe, I don't know. Now, maybe she'd want to take it out back for target practice, her eyes searching for figures on the horizon. Why are you telling me now?–I ask my husband. I ask, even though I know why he's telling me, the secret of it burning me like a brand. Now, I will see the gun hanging on our wall in the first act, aching, aching to go off in the third. The outsideman is gone for now, but he could come back. There's more than marijuana in the garage. Just in case. His face pressed to our window at night. His steps in the hall. His hands reaching for, what? For my baby? Okay, I say, nevermind, okay. Our baby is still sleeping. The house is still, so we climb together on top of the mattress and he holds me. I put my head on his chest and listen to his heart. Most accidents occur in the home, you know, I say, with firearms. I know, he says. He didn't buy the gun. He was anti-guns, before, seeing the holes they ripped in bodies in the city. Feeding the men that left missing pieces of themselves on the sidewalk. Gunshots. We used to be famous for gunshots, our city, now the whole world is. Can you even fire a gun?–I ask him and he shrugs. He could if he had to. I could if I had to. Now it's there, that iron-hot secret, and I will never not know it's waiting.

IN THE MIDDLE OF THE DESERT WE TILT OUR heads up to the sky. Even now, I hear your thoughts. Remember when we were fourteen and we cut the palms of our hands with safety scissors and put our blood together and promised to be there for each other? Is that why your thoughts are still addressed to me? After all this time? Because that's how far the magic power went? Sting of a surface wound. I think of our blood, pooling, swirling, as I look out at the night sky. There is no black blacker than the space between stars. I open my mouth because I want it to fall into me. Megan grabs my wrist and I look down. A couple people are staring, but I'm saved from scrutiny because the preacher man has started up again. We must face up to who we are, he bellows. Loud. Like a foghorn on a cargo ship. I used to hear them sometimes. I wondered what they sounded like to whales. If they sounded like bigger, scarier, metal whales. If the fish had any idea what we were doing there. I've lost the thread again. You know, it doesn't surprise me that there's a gun in the garage. There are guns all over the desert. They pop up like a new breed of succulent. Most useless since the bullets ran out. But, it took a long time for all of the bullets in that Super Walmart to get used up. I think of Megan's brother's feet dangling. He wouldn't have dangled if he'd had a gun. WE HAVE TO FACE UP TO WHO WE ARE the preacher man yells loud enough that I see him again. His shirt white against the black of the lightless desert at night. I wish I had eyes like a nocturnal animal. Flashing disks of silver caught on camera. He opens his mouth and screams. Amazing. The people around me open their mouths and scream too. The sound of it is like a hurricane. Remember when storms used to come? Or does it still storm on your mountain? It either storms too much or not at all now. Either way is deadly. SCREAM the preacher man commands and it's not unlike what I wanted to do anyway, so I tilt my head back and open my throat. The scream that comes out of me echoes with the weight of the ocean. Megan screams high, like a kestrel, a smaller raptor. Around us, everyone's scream sounds different, has a different color, a different texture. It's like those movies when demons come out of people in billowing vomits of gray smoke, but instead of gray the smoke is yellow and red and green and purple. SCREAM OUT YOUR SINS TO THE SKY. It's kind of fun, I won't lie. I might have gone to church more if it had all been like this. I ball my hands into fists at the sky and scream out the bellow of a dying whale. Deep and dark and full of water. When I'm done, it seems like the rest of the people are also done, spent, panting. Lots of people have their hands on their knees. There is a silence like the blackness between stars. So deep. We all turn our head to the preacher man, awaiting his next command.

For the rest of the morning—the rest of the hurry up, slow down, brush hair and teeth and pick me up and put me down and feed me, feed us, feed us—I am thinking about the gun. The gun in the garage glowing in my mind as my nephews run around shrieking, throwing pillows. Boys!–my sister says, sharp, but they don't listen anymore. They've figured out that there aren't any consequences now. Not after THE CATASTROPHE. We survived. My sister turns up the radio. It says that the fires are out. It says that, in some communities, neighbors are poking their heads out of their burrows and scenting the air. It says they are gathering water, food, supplies. The violence is diminishing. The bullet casings are all spent. The rage has ebbed. They are gathering donations. They are eating those donations. They are finding wood and paint and nails and building over the holes in their lives. What do you think the house looks like now?–My mother asks. We look at our hands. No one wants to tell her what they think the house looks like. My mother is house-proud. Freshly painted, white, flowers, blooms, scented sweet, buzzing bees. Orderly, orderly, nice. I don't want to tell her that it's a blackened shell of what it once was. That teenagers with spray paint, at best, have covered it with neon penises and anarchist symbols.

Or, maybe, worse, another family has moved in. A squatters family with hollow eyes and yellow teeth. Maybe the dad looks like the outsideman? And then, a flash, the gun in the garage. The man, not dead, tentless, wandering around outside. The distance between them, the gun and the man, is vibrating with such anticipatory energy I can't take it. I want to get the gun, find the man, and shoot him. Then it will be over. I'm sure the house has gotten messed up a little, my husband says, wanting to be gentle, thinking of my mother's windchimes hanging from wrought-iron shepherd's hooks in the front yard. The weeds are probably out of control, my sister says. As if that's what's wrong, overgrowth. But, maybe we can still go back, my mother says, the light of our old lives bright in her eyes. She sees us, on a summer evening five years ago, all together, all laughing, slapping the mosquitos at our ankles into bloody smears. Before. My mother's face whispers at us all, in the lullaby whispers that were our first introduction to language and love. Maybe, my husband says, but I say nothing. There's a gun in the garage. My baby wants me to pick her up, so I hoist her to my hip and look into her grave little human eyes. After, her eyes say. There is only after for her.

THE PREACHER MAN IS STILL FOR A MOMENT and then he's beaming and we're all beaming and everybody laughs. We laugh like we just screamed. It takes over my whole body, maybe it's a group psychosis. I've never seen Megan laugh this hard. It takes a long time for the laughter to peter off. We'll sleep here tonight, the preacher man says, once the crowd has quieted down to the occasional guffaw and hiccup. We'll sleep under these stars together, and I'll tell you right now, I'll promise you this: we're going to wake up to rain. I admire the calm certitude with which the congregation settles itself into the sand. Like ghost crabs digging holes, families stake out parts of the desert for themselves. Megan and I make our way a little to the east, to the sunrise. We lay on our backs and she doesn't ask me if I think it's going to rain. Instead, she says, I think I screamed up a lot of pain. Her voice is harsh, she puts her hand to her throat and massages it with her slim fingers. She screamed roughness into her voice, but she feels good, she says. It was like tar in my belly, Megan says. I was thinking about my mother and my brother and how my father rumbled out of town before all this, before everything. I reach out and take her hand. We look up at the sky. Do you think my father's safe?—Megan whispers, and I shrug. Maybe? Who can say?—I say and she nods. I know he's dead. It makes me think of my own father. Of his yellow-flecked spittle, of the fear in his eyes. He was the first person to respond to my power with that fear, but not the last. I had to get careful about who I would let see it. Once, I pressed my lips to a little boy's mouth after dragging him, limp, from the ocean. I could feel his mother's eyes above my head, worrying their way into my skull, so with my breath, just to be sure, I sent out a little pulse of light. Just a bit. The boy sat up like a rocket, coughing and pounding the sand with his fists. His mother looked at me funny, didn't say thank you, but she didn't slap me the way a waitress did once after I, mistaking everything about our early-morning conversations, reached out and pulsed a little light into her temple to take the worry away. Don't touch me, she said, and it sounded like my father. What do you think, Megan, I ask. About what? About, you know, me? We look up at the sky and it is bright, too bright, I miss clouds, I miss obstruction, obfuscation. I don't like how everything is so bald and plain these days. Megan laughs and crinkles up her nose laughing. I like you a lot, she says. You're a strong person. You're strong like the trunk of a tree. I like that. Like the trunk of a tree. I let my eyes be dazzled by the stars and I forget my father's face, the waitress' voice, the look that mother gave me. I forget the girl with the multi-colored markers and the clack of pool balls in a bar. I become a tree in the desert, rooted to the sand. Spreading out and trying to send my pulse of light to a living thing that will appreciate it. As I drift off to sleep, I even forget that it's supposed to rain.

The boys want to go outside so badly and I can't tell them not to because then I'd have to tell them of the outsideman and how I know about the gun in the garage. I should be mad that my family kept the gun a secret from me, but I'm not. I'm happy they realized I wouldn't want to know. I can't live long with the anxiety that something like a gun in the garage causes without lashing out, taking it out on other people. I take a deep breath, one, two, three, four and let it out, one, two, three, four. A nice therapist in a yellow cardigan taught me that trick a week before THE CATASTROPHE made us leave our homes. I told her sometimes I couldn't sleep. I told her that I'd sleep for a few hours and then wake up in the middle of the night to worry intensely about something. What something?—she asked. Anything. The dripping faucet in the bathroom, my baby dying, the house filling with silent carbon monoxide, my husband getting shot at work, car accidents, fires, the fact that the cicadas just come out of the ground and we act like that's normal, the things we'll look away from, the things I close my eyes to. She put up her hand, or I could have kept going all day. My husband suggested this nice therapist's office, around the corner from our apartment and painted pink like an Easter egg. He said they were good at working with women. Women are anxious, women watch their babies grow and the storm clouds gather.

Try this trick, the nice therapist said, in, one, two, three, four, out, one, two, three, four. At best, that's going to clear my head for two seconds. Two seconds is a start, she said. The blue chain from which her reading glasses dangled. The framed photograph of a yellow lab on her wall beside her framed diplomas. The thought hits me sudden, a swoop, a stab, my therapist is dead. In a fire, in a plague. In, one, two, three, four, in, one, two, three, four. Sure, let's go outside, I tell the boys. I smile and it's easy to. We all go. It's our main form of entertainment and we start thinking of it as our path and our woods. As if we paid any money or fought any battle to earn them or keep them. Halfway through the circle, I can tell now by the length of time we've been walking, I see him leaning against a tree. I blink, I think I'm imagining it. One, two, three, four, but no, he's there. Emaciated, filthy. What happened to him? Something must have happened to him since he slept under the porch. I squint and think I see a wound over his eye, blood drying on his forehead. I reach over and grab my husband's hand, my baby dangling from the carrier on his chest, but when my husband looks up, the outsideman moves, swift, behind the tree trunk, like a shadow. He let me see him, just me. I'm the king of the forest!—my beautiful blonde nephew roars, glowing with power, hoisting a tree branch over his head.

WHEN WE WAKE, IT HASN'T RAINED. OF COURSE
it hasn't. Did you think it would? I can tell that Megan
thought it would. She wakes in confusion. I want to laugh at
the congregation and their misplaced faith, but the wrinkle
between Megan's eyebrows, so lost, makes me too sad. The
preacher man gets frantic. He doesn't understand. His
calculations. His certainty. The desert is dry and windy.
Sand bites at the corners of our eyes. The wind shushes the
preacher man's howls. The fascinating thing is the silence. The
congregation greets the dry day in silence. My joints pop as I
stand, reach down, help Megan to her feet. People brush the
sand off the front of their clothes and look at each other and
shrug. They shrug. As if they knew it was a long shot. As if,
what are you going to do? The preacher man seems devastated.
He is shouting at the sky again, but he's so upset his words
slur and I can't quite make them out. One comes through
crystal clear, though: why. Why, why, why?–the preacher
man asks. His body looks smaller, like he has shrunk without
authority. His congregation begins to leave. They leave him
there in the desert. No one walks over and puts their hand
on his shoulder. No one hugs him and tells him it's all right,
we all make mistakes. The congregation turns, as one sandy
body, and walks out of the desert, as dry as they were when
they walked in. I feel bad for the wild-eyed preacher man.
I feel like he's coming face-to-face for the first time in his
life with helplessness. You know I've been helpless. I know
you've been helpless and Megan's been helpless, and even the
girl with the colored markers, from time to time, has been
helpless. But this man, he must've walked through his life
feeling the surge of power in his every step. Like a little boy

124

with a stick for a sword, running through his family's woods. And now? Now he's on his knees in the desert, fists raised to the sky. I walk over to him. Megan watches, amused, from a distance. Hey, now, hey, I say like he's a bucking horse. He kind of looks like a bucking horse, actually. The whites of his eyes roll wild. Why?–he asks me. He looks at me as if my face is the sky and he asks me the same question. I was so sure, why? But, I have no answer he'd like. I could tell him nobody else was convinced it'd work, but I don't. I put a hand on his forehead and pulse a little light into him. That quiets him down. I turn and take Megan's arm and together we walk back home. What are they gonna do now?–I ask her and she bites her lip. I can tell she doesn't want to tell me and that starts my nerves jangling. Megan? They won't do it, she says. It's just talk. Talk about what? Talk about . . . you know. And then I know, this was it. This was the absolute, last, final plea to the universe. The last letter to big daddy, if you're there, save us. How are they planning on doing it? I ask, wondering if I can stop them. Wondering if there's enough life in my body, enough light, to stretch it out that thin. I dunno, Megan says, but I can tell she does know. She's more shaken than I thought she'd be. Well, when is it, at least? Maybe we can stop them. They keep pushing it back, Megan says, squinting up at the roof of the trailer. She's splayed out, still sandy, like a starfish where she sleeps. I'm watching her like she's going to dissolve any moment. Dog rests his snout on her belly. Megan closes her eyes and waits. I understand what your therapist was trying to say. Sometimes it takes four seconds to make a choice. This is gonna sound dumb, but, Megan says, her eyes still closed with shame, I thought it was going to rain.

I see him everywhere now. And it's crazy because now is when the reports come in that THE CATASTROPHE is starting to ebb, like a wave retreating over sand. Riptide. I see his head outlined against my bedroom window. A silhouette of the outsideman. I freeze and wait, and keep my hand on my sleeping baby's chest, but he moves off. My sister leans her head into our bedroom at night to tell us that the power is back on in the city. Our city? We whisper because even before THE CATASTROPHE, our city was never known for its competent government or stellar services. Our city, my sister says. I think about the orange-hued streetlights on my block, blinking back to life one by one. Some must have burnt out. I think of men in reflective vests on cranes replacing the bulbs, turning the lights back on in their sockets. In the morning, as I'm flipping the kitten calendar to a new month, I see the outsideman against the treeline. His clothes are filthy, but his hair is white, white, against the backdrop of green. I freeze again. I'm a mama deer in front of a Range Rover. If I stay still, maybe he's not there, watching us. The thought of him watching us makes my throat feel tight. I raise my hand to grasp it, but then he steps back into the shadows and I can breathe. My sister turns on her radio and my mother says, no radio at breakfast! But it's the familiar jingle of our pre-catastrophe radio. We recognize the man's voice, our city's accent, he sounds flustered and elated. Hello? Hello?–the man in the radio says. I can't believe I'm back on the air. It's so good to be back on the air. That last rain storm swept through the city and carried so much garbage out. The streets are clean and the lights are on. My family freezes at the breakfast table, smiles plastered to our faces. We can't believe it. Can we believe it? The sound of gunshots, but there are no more bullets now. The radio says we've shot every shot, and now if we want to murder, we'll have to do it with our hands. Except for the gun in the garage. It burns like I've swallowed something hot, but then it recedes. If there are no bullets anymore and the lights are back on and the streets are clean, then. Maybe we can go home?–my mother says. My brother-in-law frowns and fiddles with the dial, looking for his doomsday radio. We still have so much food stored up. There's no reason to be hasty. No reason except for the strong pull of wanting what we had before. The sad-voiced men on my brother-in-law's preferred radio channel are talking about the rain. It's raining and raining like I've never seen. The earth was so thirsty and dirty and now, now there's water cleaning everything, clear water, cleaning the dirt away. My brother-in-law frowns harder, but a spark of wonder lights up his eyes. The boys pick up on the note of hope in our voices, and so do the dogs, I think. They stand at the back door, waiting to be released into the green. The green grass, the green trees, the silent movement of the sparse herd of deer. Maybe we can go home?–I ask my husband with my eyes, and he can read my thoughts, that's how long we've been married, and he smiles, half-sad, and shrugs. He'll be the last to believe it. My sister opens the door and the boys and dogs bolt. She turns the radio back to our local DJ, the one whose voice we know. We stand in silence and watch the boys and the dogs run, boundless energy, boundless hope. Just over the hill, I see the outsideman, leaning against a tree, looking back.

THE CONGREGATION KILLED THEMSELVES LAST night. There are no more bullets, your radio is right, so they drank poison. Something viscous. I held Megan's hand in the morning when it was so quiet and I knew. Besides us and the pilgrims, the church people were the last people left in the desert and I could feel their dead bodies, mouths ringed with sticky blue poison, pressing into the sand. A great silence. I didn't want Megan to know, but she took one look at my face and said, you can feel it, can't you? I nodded because I don't believe in lying to people, especially not family, not even to save their feelings. Her face crumpled and then just as quickly smoothed itself out. I told them, sure, yeah. I told them I'd be there when they did it, she said. I thought I would sneak out without you noticing, and then I'd be there with them at the end. I'm glad you weren't, I said. I put on a pair of sturdy denim overalls. I have a shovel, the one I used to bury the nonperishables. We walked to the old bar that used to be the church. A silent walk. Their bodies were waiting for us, bloated, but smelling of the chemicals they drank, not death. Their eyes were open. They stared. I'm gonna throw up, Megan said. Listen, I said, hefting my shovel in my palm, instead of burying them all like this, one by one, I mean, we could just burn this place to the ground. Isn't that, I don't know, desecration—disrespectful?–Megan asked, she fiddled with her hair and rubbed her forehead and didn't look at the dead bodies, folded nicely, not sprawled. They didn't look like they were in any pain. They looked like they made a decision together. They chose to spread their bodies across the bar, across the floor, clustered together in family groups. Friends close to friends. They held hands. Their vacant eyes pointed towards each other's faces. They might have been smiling before their muscles relaxed. I don't think so, I said, it's a way to keep them all together, anyway. Megan bit her lip. I could tell she was still nauseous, but dead things never bothered me. Not the rabbit, not the whale, not the congregation, who walked calmly to their deaths, fulfilling their half of a bargain. Maybe they were at peace because after the rain didn't come they thought God wanted them dead. It's not an unreasonable thing, looking at the world, to think God wants us dead. Okay, Megan said. Then we had to figure out how to get the place to catch. All of the booze had long since been drunk, except for the booze in the preacher man's special store. That's when we heard sniffling. The preacher man was crouched behind the bar, surrounded on all sides by his dead congregation. He didn't drink the poison. He was alive. Don't hurt me!–was the first thing he said when Megan and I peeked over the bar and looked down on him in his little fortress. Why would we hurt you?–I asked, but I saw the rage flare in Megan's eyes. He'd made this promise for them. The least he could do was die beside them. Maybe he'll see them, like you see your outsideman, everywhere he goes. Their long-sleeved dresses, their uncut hair, the calm certitude in their dead eyes. Their chemical-blue lips. I can help you light it on fire, the preacher-man says, wiping his palms on his pants, avoiding his congregation's empty stares.

I spend the rest of the morning trying to look cheerful. I try to let the joy and hope of the moment seep into my eyes, but I can't quite manage it. I'm faking, and everyone can tell. My sister frowns at me. She thinks I'm being stubborn in the face of overwhelming evidence. She turns up the radio and we hear the astonished glee of the radio announcer saying things like, the water's back on! We have reports of food trucks moving into the city and surrounding counties! I lower my eyes. My husband feels sympathetic and touches my lower back, my belly, my shoulders. Little touches to say I'm here, but I know he's feeling hopeful too. I can't take their scrutiny anymore, I never liked being the odd one out, so I walk out onto the green lawn. To the place where the outsideman pitched his tent. I lie down on the grass and spread my arms and legs out like a starfish. Like the points on a compass. The sun burns my eyelids red. In, one, two, three, four. I'm just afraid of change. Out, one, two, three, four. All I want now is for everything to stay the same. I want us safe and hidden from the world. I no longer care if we are kind, decent people. I want us invisible to THE CATASTROPHE. I feel a disturbance in the grass at my side, and turn my head. My mother, in her pink cashmere sweater, pearls, has stretched herself out on the ground beside me. She's closed her eyes and tilted her face up to the sun. You're going to get dirty, I tell her and she nods. Sure, she says. We're all dirty. We lie together in silence, and this is my mother's way of telling me that she understands. Why should we give up a safe place, a quiet place, full of food, to go back to a home that might not even exist anymore? Why risk it? Eventually, my mother says, we'll run out of rice. But not for a while, I murmur, thinking of my big pot simmering on the stove. Eventually, someone is going to need antibiotics. Are there even any more antibiotics in the world?—I ask. Silence. We're not sure. Eventually, my mother says, her mind focused on a time that's years and years in the future. A time after we lay her body to rest in a green field and grow flowers on her grave. Eventually, she says, we'll need other people again. I feel my face snarl. Other people are the problem, I say. The sun is making me see spots, rainbows. I close my eyes again, lie beside my mother. I bought myself this necklace, my mother says, running the pads of her fingers over the soft shine of her pearls. Before I met your father. I bought this necklace even though I didn't have any money because I knew exactly the kind of life I wanted to have. I had to believe it was possible for me. Then she doesn't say anything else. She takes my hand like I'm still a child, and I feel very small, like a seed of some greater tree. We lie in the sun together for a long, long time.

YOU'RE RIGHT, WE'RE ALL THE PROBLEM. AND good for you for realizing that you could strangle someone if you wanted to. I know I could. I've been in a couple of bar fights, busted a knuckle on a jaw, tasted other people's blood on my lips. I liked it and I didn't. I liked it in the moment, but I felt bad afterwards. Megan is worn out from the violence of the day. I keep thinking about a sea of convulsing bodies, just before they die of poison. I hope it wasn't too painful—although, I know that kind of chemical causes internal organs to liquify. It must have hurt a lot. Dog sticks close to Megan. Even when she walks out into the dark desert alone waving her hand behind her head to tell me not to follow. I hear his collar jingling, even after they disappear into the darkness. I would follow at a distance, just to be safe, but I know she doesn't want me there. She wants to look up at the stars alone, and she wants to ask why. It's dangerous to ask questions like that—it can lead to despair. I let myself back into the trailer, and boil some tea. I stare at Giles in his terrarium, and he stares back. I'm nervous about what Megan might do to herself, but I know it's important to trust her—to have her see that I trust her. She's gone for a long time, and I drink my tea and read my own leaves. You want a home, the leaves tell me, like they're mocking me. Is that such a bad thing to want? Isn't it what you want too? What everyone normal wants? I know I'm not normal, but

I can still want something ordinary. I'll give up this useless spark inside of me if it means I can have ten years of peace. Remember the school girl outfits? Everyone the same. You and I were the same then; we were two halves of a whole girl. Can't we have that again? Can't we have ivy and thick walls and trees? What a luxury it was, to not have to bury food, to not have to press our ears to the radio speakers. It occurs to me that I could take Megan with me. We could pack up the trailer and go. Somewhere safe. Is anywhere safe anymore? I would find a safe place, for her. But, what if she carries the catastrophe in her mind? We become unsafe places. Sleep bears down on me. A heavy weight. Funny, I can usually keep myself awake all night, spinning scenarios in the shell inside of me. I have less quiet now, less imagination, more worry, and my body is exhausted with it. Maybe I never appreciated it before—how tired you must be from all your loving. One baby would wipe me out for good. I lay down on my bed and try to stay awake until Megan comes back. All I need is the jingle of Dog's collar in the night, and I'll know she chose to stay. I don't want to wake up and start the morning calling out to an empty horizon. Fear keeps me half-awake until I hear it. A happy little chuffing bark. Dog and Megan slip back into the trailer smelling of sand and night wind. I don't open my eyes. I let her think she's snuck past me. They curl up together, two animals seeking comfort, and before I drift off to sleep I hear them snoring together, one breath, in and out. She came back. Just like that.

At night, everything is blue. I stare at the ceiling and listen to my husband and baby breathe. At first, it was too dark out here. I'd missed the orange sulfur lights of my block in the city. The flashing lights of sirens. Headlights rolling by. Now, I think I could be a creature of the dark. Huge eyes, reflective, like a possum. I hear a whispering and a crackle coming from the kitchen. I think of my sister and mother, their heads bent together, talking about what to do with the red tent. Indignant—I am an adult, I can be included in the discussions, even if they are distasteful. I step out, barefeet, into the living room, but the noise is just the radio. The rest of the room is empty. My brother-in-law must've left the speakers on. After dinner, he fiddled with the knobs, trying to get his radio of despair back on. It'd disappeared. Replaced with the radio of renewed hope. My brother-in-law felt lost without his melancholy radio. He searched and searched for a signal before giving up and going to bed. I put my ear right next to the speaker and I imagine I can hear your voice crackling over the wire. Maye it's a trap, your voice says, with all the heavy wisdom it had even when we were teenagers. I wish you'd waited for me to come back. I think you'd know what to do in this situation, now. I press my ear so hard to the speaker that it burns. Somewhere, underneath the static, I think I hear my brother-in-law's favorite DJ, warning, don't give in to hope, don't give in, it's a scam. Maybe that's just what I want to hear. Out of the corner of my eye, I think I see someone moving outside the house. It's him. It has to be.

There are no dogs, they're sleeping with their happy masters, basking in the dreams of a new life, a regrowth. I bet they're chasing squirrels in their dreams. I bet in a dog's dream, there are still bees. I unstick my head from the speaker and go to the garage. Fine. If he wants me to do it. If he's lurking because he wants me to do it, then, fine. The garage smells like mildew and marijuana. I can feel it on my fingers—sticky. The gun is where my husband said it would be. It's loaded, I think. I don't know anything about guns, but it's heavy. It shines. I think it could be beautiful, if it weren't so ugly. It makes me think of that boy you pushed into the lake, the boy that went to jail for murder—but I only raped her, he said. I only raped her and left her to die. Now, there are no guns on the streets of our city. Or, there are guns, but no bullets. Guns are useless clicking L shapes of metal without their bullets. It makes me happy for a moment, but then I imagine the streets red with blood punched out of noses, stabbed out of bellies. We're obsessed with blood, it'll run. I take the gun with me outside. I stand in the dark. I wait for the shadow to move across the moon, to move across me. I don't believe the radio. I don't believe that we can all go back. Go back to my parents' suburban house, white brick and ivy. Go back to my rowhouse, alley cats, earnest social workers, methadone clinics. Go back to when we were fourteen and cutting our palms to swear our allegiance. I haven't had a friend willing to shed blood for me since then. In the dark, I think I hear footsteps. I think I hear his footsteps coming closer, closer, closer.

IN THE TRAILER, I HAVE TO KEEP MEGAN FROM falling away from me. She's angry and she's sad and I can see the two warring it out on her angular face. She wants to run, she can't imagine running. I feel it all in purple waves radiating off her body. Dog feels it too. He snuffles at her ankles, but it isn't enough to get her frown to unbend. And I want to tell her that I'd stay like this, woman, Dog, woman, in my trailer, her on the futon, me on the bed, forever. I want to tell her that we could breathe together inside this small space and let the world end outside and that would be fine. Don't worry about ropes or pills or poison. Don't worry about the human instinct for survival bent backwards on itself in despair. Half of our longing is destruction. You going to stay around here? Megan asks. What do you mean? I keep my eyes on the ceiling, I don't like the way she said you and not we. I mean, you could hitch the trailer to your old truck, drive somewhere where it rains. Somewhere green. A city? The outskirts of a city. For a moment, I see it in a flash, woman, Dog, woman, on the outskirts of a city. Lights flickering back on. Flames doused by a light rain shower. Music playing, food smelling on the stove. Someone is humming, there's a baby, there's more babies, there's life and not death, not for a while anyway, not until it's welcome. I don't know, I tell Megan. I can't imagine where I'd go. It's a lie. I imagine the ocean, I imagine the forest, but I'm afraid of the living things there. I'm afraid of what people see in me. I don't know what the point is, even, Megan says. She starts chewing on the end of one of her braids and it makes me feel better, like she's doing something so normal that maybe this day is all normal. Like maybe, if I close my eyes, I don't see their lips ringed with blue poison. I don't see the preacher man, eyes dry, watching them burn. The point of what?–I ask. Of life, Megan says. At this point, I'm hanging on with pure stubbornness. I laugh, I can't help it. She sounds like a cactus, like a tumbleweed. Maybe pure stubbornness is the point of life, I say. You know, I never heard from that man again. That man and his redheaded waitress. I just wanted a baby, which is insane, if you think about it. A baby born into the apocalypse. And she sounds so sad that I can't help but say it—the radio says it's getting better. I don't know why, I don't know if I even believe it, this signal broadcast over the desert, invisible signal filling up the corners of the atmosphere. It's getting better, the signal says. You can trust again, the signal says. There are no bullets left. Do you believe that?–Megan asks and I shrug, I try not to look at her, but I can't help it. She and Dog are tangled up now in my heart. The whole bruised purple mess of us. What's the alternative?–I ask.

Shooting a gun is easier than I thought it'd be. Maybe all that masculine talk made me think that it was something that required muscle, that the kickback would hurt me, that I didn't have the strength to pull the trigger. But, gun technology has come a long way, I guess, from those early days. A baby could have pulled this trigger. My baby. It feels good to pull, like scratching a red itch, an itch I had at the back of my mind from the time I heard my husband say there's a gun in the garage. It feels so good, release, to point the gun towards the shape moving towards me in the dark. Overhead, the moon shines bright. I hit the shadow, easy. It falls. The sound is the give away. I wish this gun was silent. My husband comes running out of the house first, then my sister and brother-in-law the boys, then my parents, their poor old knees, wake up, spring up in the way a gunshot can make a person spring. I have one more moment of feeling proud, like a warrior, and released, like I have fulfilled the inevitable, before the screaming gets me. What the fuck what the fuck what the fuck, my husband murmurs like a prayer. Inside, I can hear my baby crying and I feel that tug, that pull at the very center of me, but I can't move. What did you shoot? My nephews are excited. They run over to the shadow, crumpled in on itself in the blue grass of night. Get back here!–my sister yells and, for once, the boys obey her. Maybe they respect death. I saw a shadow, I say. I saw a shadow out my window. My husband jogs over to the corpse, the dead thing I made dead, and I see the relief on his face, so plain, even in the dark. It's just a deer, he calls. The anxiety seeps from my family's shoulders then. Just a deer. But, that's not what I meant to shoot. I think of the mama deer, her soft fawn side-stepping, ginger, on those pinprick legs. No, it wasn't a deer, I whisper, but it is. It's the mama deer, poking her head out of the green leaves. Just a deer, my husband says like he's relieved. I drop the gun. The itch is gone and instead there's a hole there, like I scratched a hole into myself, into the deer, into everything. I'm sorry, I'm sorry, I say.

LISTEN, I TELL MEGAN, WE CAN PACK UP THE trailer. We can hitch it to your truck, we can take the food I've buried. We can take Dog. I want the defiance to come back into her eyes. I don't like how empty they seem, like the congregation, blue-lipped and burning. That poor deer. Did you think you were shooting a man? Did you think that was better? Where would we even go?—Megan asks, her voice flat and I hate it. It makes me think of my mother's flat voice, before she died, and how flat the earth was above her grave. Her stone was cold under my hands. I guess my father is dead now too, and that blonde boy you loved in high school, and every cat I've ever seen. We could go to the ocean, I say, because that's the place I think of, waves crashing, saying home, home, come home. I don't even think about the girl with the multi-colored markers or the things she drew on my arms. You don't like the ocean. I bet the beach is covered in dead whales now, Megan says. I want to fight her, to punch a hole in the trailer, just to feel something good for a minute, but I'm weak. My body is weak from months of canned beans, and, worse than that, something, my light, the pulsing, small, power inside me is weak. I think of the preacher man, how he hid behind the bar. Okay, we can go to the mall, then, I say. The malls are all burned out, Megan says, they were the first things to burn. We'll find a mall that still has a Bed, Bath & Beyond. Remember Bed, Bath, & Beyond? Remember the chemical smell of Sweet Pea? And we can get a big comfy bed and blankets, we can eat soft pretzels and build our own teddy bears with little fabric hearts sewn inside. The mall doesn't exist anymore,

Megan says, but she's not even angry. She's just saying. She's right. Okay, fine, we can go somewhere. We can drive and see what's there. We can drive until we hit rain. I'm desperate for her to agree. Megan sighs. She pulls her hair back into a severe bun. She's trying to keep herself from sucking on the ends of her braids, she thinks it's a juvenile habit. I don't want her to stop it. I don't want this sadness to change her, though it has, it has changed even the earth under our feet. Even you, shooting a deer. You who cried when horses died in movies. Shooting a deer because you thought it was a man. Okay, Megan says, she rubs her eyes with her open palms. Okay, we can drive, okay. I'm so relieved, I decide to ignore the shape of her mouth, the frown of it. Dog thumps his tail once because I'm smiling, but he keeps his ears down because Megan is sad. There's no one left in the desert. If the preacher man caught a ride with a pilgrim then we are the last people out here, the last people in the dark. We can pack up today, Megan says, but I want to get drunk tonight. I want to get super drunk and spread out on my back in the desert and look up at the stars. I have to think of the congregation, sleeping like kittens curled together on the sand, waiting for the rain that never came. That's fair, I say. I'm thinking of how to get the cans of nonperishables into the trailer, how to get enough gas to power us to wherever the woman with the tinted windows was heading, to whatever the city and what's beyond the city has become now. Hey, I reach out and grab Megan's hand. It's the first time I've ever grabbed her hand like this and she smiles down at our fingers intertwined. I know, she says, not looking at me, I know.

My family tries to make a joke of me shooting the deer. Annie Oakley. Lizzie Borden, though that was an axe. Bambi's mom. I feel sick to my stomach picturing the ballerina arc of the deer's dead neck. My husband puts his hand on me when they start making fun. Trying to pulse some love into my skin. I shouldn't have shot. It's like a dream. I woke up, pressed my ear to the radio, heard static, and fetched the gun. I can remember, so clearly, wanting to shoot the outsideman. Now, I'm not even sure I've been seeing him. What if it was just a shadow, a broken branch leaning up against a tree? The wind? What if he was never here at all? But, I remember the red tent, covered in mud and twigs. Later, my husband goes into the woods and shoots the rest of the bullets into the ground. Muffled boom boom boom click. Now, I couldn't shoot anyone even if I wanted to. My mother agrees that the gun was overkill. We do dangerous things when we're afraid, she says. We do dangerous things, I think, like flee. It makes me wonder about the old neighborhood, about the rats and the garbage, the recycling they stopped collecting. My husband said recycling was a sham anyway, had been for years, that they sold it to China and it wobbled in giant mounds, tricking birds into eating it and choking on plastic wire. We were all culpable then, but the culpability was far away. This is here. This is in my hands. Deer blood. That's why the jokes. They're cutting me slack, admitting that everyone's nerve endings are fried and it's okay that I went and got the gun at night to shoot at shadows. They would have done the same thing. In different circumstances, in a million acid-erosion ways, they've all done what I've done. It turned out okay because I only killed a deer. My brother-in-law and husband put on rubber gloves and carried the deer carcass into the woods. The boys wanted to poke it with sticks, stick their fingers into its oozing eyeballs. Children are savage. They wanted to desecrate the corpse, but we didn't let them. We told them it was a mistake. We could have eaten it if any of us knew how to butcher a deer. My sister works in finance, my husband in the non-profit sector, I used to work in education. Used to. All of our jobs evaporated when THE CATASTROPHE came. All of the things that make our lives, not on the mountain, make sense. We were a part of something that made it possible for us to survive even though we have no idea how to butcher a deer. I can open cans. Non-perishables. I open the cans to make pasta and veggies for lunch. Beans. The boys eat it and pretend that it's deer. I'm a mountain lion, my redheaded nephew says. A sign I saw once hiking with my husband: IN CASE OF MOUNTAIN LION ATTACK FIGHT BACK AGGRESSIVELY. I laughed at the time, told everyone I'd just die. But, I imagine the claws, the teeth on my skin. I imagine snapping a muscular neck. The outsideman is skinny, maybe I don't need a gun to kill him. This thought sends a shiver through my whole body. When did I decide that I had to kill him? I haven't seen his body lounging, walking, sleeping, waiting, all day. If he's real, maybe he's finally, finally, gone away.

MEGAN AND I IN THE DESERT, STARING UP AT the night sky. Dog walking protective circles around us. It's night. So dark, so dark. You think it gets dark like this in the city now?–Megan asks. We haven't decided, but she figures we'll have to end up somewhere close to the city. We'll run out of food. We'll have to learn things, like butchering a deer. I don't think my body would starve. I can feel the faint glow of my power, pulsing, underneath my skin. It's returning from its despair at the congregation's sticky blue mouths. I don't know, I tell her. I don't know how much electricity is left. I don't know if there are parts of the city, walled-off, I'm sure, that hum with all the excess of ourselves ten years ago. Remember ten years ago? I was gone, but I still heard your thoughts in my mind like you were sitting on my shoulder. I thought, maybe this is what having a twin sister is like. I pricked my forefinger with a safety pin until it bled, wondering if I'd hear you think, *ouch*. Dog has decided we're not in danger, so he lies down at Megan's feet. She is his lady and now she is also mine. You think there's food in the city?–Megan asks. Who knows, I say. What I don't tell her is that, yes. I think there's too much food in the city. Preserved, unperishable. So many people have died that what's left of us can live in their shell, like a hermit crab crawling from shelter to shelter on the seafloor. We'll grow to fit, until the next collapse. You think there's violence?–Megan asks. There are no bullets left, I say, even though I'm not that confident about it. They say there are no more bullets, but can't men just make more? Wouldn't that be one of the first things to be made anew? Swords into ploughshares, Megan murmurs. Then Dog gets up and shakes his shaggy shoulders. I hear, rather than see, him run towards the trailer. It's so dark but there's nothing to stumble over. Dog!–Megan shouts, but he doesn't turn, which surprises me. Usually, her voice can bring him back in an instant. He's barking and that's when I see the headlights. Even before she stops the car and climbs out of the driver's seat, even before Megan and I get up, shake the dust off of our clothes and walk toward her, even before Dog, uncertain, raises his lips in a silent growl, I know who it is. I wonder if she has multi-colored markers in her pocket.

FOUR

Lord, I confess I want clarity of catastrophe but not the
    catastrophe.
Like everyone else, I want storm I can dance in.
I want an excuse to change my life.

Franny Choi, *Catastrophe is Next to Godliness*

My husband thinks I've been under too much stress. He puts his fingers on my face gentle, says I look tired. I used to hate being told I looked tired when what it meant was I had forgotten to put on mascara. Now, it feels like being seen. Yes, I am tired. I am more tired than I've ever been even though we've been inactive for so long. Maybe I'll sleep?—I ask, but my husband frowns. Sleeping in the middle of the day is a bad sign. It means something has gone off track in my mind. But I feel clearer since shooting the deer. I feel like I had to shoot something, and now that I have I can see far past the horizon. Maybe you should read a book? You used to love reading books. He's right, I used to have piles of books by my bedside. I used to listen to audiobooks while nursing my baby. I used to order books from independent publishers from independent bookstores. I read the weirdest, smallest books. I read a book about a woman collecting penises, metaphorically; the cover blossomed with mushrooms. I read books wherein people worried about what the purpose of their life was, not about fires or floods or shooting deer in the night. All those malaisemen cheating on their wives. All those younger women eating it up. Oh god, the delicate bend of that deer's neck. Okay, I say, I think there are some books in the study. So, I go. The baby watches me and I feel that tug, but it's looser. Like I'm floating away from her because now I am the kind of mother, wild-eyed, who tiptoes out of her bedroom at night in search of a gun. My uncle's study has classics. Spines uncracked. Dust. Bound in the kind of red-brown leather that looks like dried cognac. Spilled. Charles Dickens. Bleak House. I sit in my uncle's wheelie chair and spin. Open to a random page. Below me my family is listening to the hopeful murmurs of the radio. My brother-in-law refuses to believe it. He's saying that he'll walk down the mountain today. Down and back up and tell us what he sees. My sister presses her lips together, doesn't tell him no, don't go, it's too dangerous. I tried to read Charles Dickens. Remember when we were school girls? Remember when I told you that all I ever wanted was to write big, heavy books. Write myself into existence with books big enough to give someone a concussion. Maybe it was irresponsible to have my longed-for baby. Maybe now, now that everything might be fine, I'll ruin her with my worry, grasping like vines at my mind. Don't go outside. At least the bullets are gone. Maybe we'll never make any more. From the study window I see my brother-in-law's long strides. He is stomping down the mountain. I watch his back until he disappears.

148

THE GIRL WITH THE MULTI-COLORED MARKERS is a woman now. She has lines at her mouth, lines at her eyes. I remember Bleak House. Remember Great Expectations? I wonder if, now that everything is ending, people will still read books that big or if they'll use them as weapons. She's smiling, smells like synthetic cherries, says howdy and means it. What are you doing here?—is the first thing I ask. Megan looks sly, out of the corner of her eye she can take us both in. I see her trying to paint a picture. Still life. Exes in the desert. She was a girl when we first met and so was I. Old enough to be a woman but still a girl. Salt on the air. The waves. I only saw the beautiful things about the beach, then. The beautiful things about her. She has perfect teeth. I thought you might need a ride out of here, she says. It's odd that she doesn't have markers in her hands. I feel like I've lied to Megan about her and also like the real version of her can't compare to the tales I've told. I mean, we have a truck and a trailer. Dog sniffs her hands. He doesn't like her as much as he likes Megan but his tail still swings from side to side. She scratches his ears without looking at him. Remember when we ran through the woods behind our houses? The woods that hadn't yet been chopped down to build more ranch-style houses. Now, I bet they're overgrown again. Think about how much of our destruction the catastrophe has undone. Maybe the mammoths and ground sloths will return. Maybe ice will creep over the land again. Everything will come back. I feel my shoulders itch for that long lost leather jacket. I'm Megan, Megan says and I realize I haven't introduced her. I took her presence for granted, as if I were expected to gesture around me and say this is the desert. There's a fire still smouldering in town, she says. It looks like it was a bar or something? She smiles at our silence, she loves silences like that, filled with pain. She has a better nose for a story than anyone I've ever met. She's wearing red lipstick and I wonder where, at the end of the world, did she get it? We don't need a ride, Megan says, louder, this time. She stops ignoring Megan, then. I can see her decide that if Megan wants to be dealt with, she must be dealt with. When she turns, I see a purple sharpie poking out of her jean pocket and it's like I'm in a different world where there are soft serve ice cream machines, taffy, seagulls, and sand crabs. I bet it's all garbage garbage garbage now. Once I swam out in the ocean to retrieve a shiny red heart-shaped balloon. It was deflated and covered in grime. I felt triumphant hauling it back to shore, but when I turned it was just the vanguard of trash swept in by a night's rain from the boardwalk above. Well, maybe I can join up with you, then?—she asks. We're safer in numbers. Megan looks at me, but I can't tell what she wants me to say. Does she want me to banish the past to the past? Does she want me to ask this woman, who was once a girl who was once cruel to me in a way I liked, to stay with us forever? We're leaving the day after tomorrow, I say. Okay, she says, that's fine. I can see Megan shift her weight from one foot to the other. Dog whines. He doesn't like her uncertainty. I can sleep in the truck, she says, hands raised, palms out, as if she comes in peace.

I watch my brother-in-law go and I wonder if he'll be back. We never had a chance to go anywhere. Our adventures in high school were to the lake. Off with boys. Down to the woods with a bottle of cheap vodka. In college, each little town in Pennsylvania had its own brand of cheap vodka. Mine was called Vladimir. It had a picture of an old Cossack on the front, stooped under the weight of his mustache. We humans have seen a lot of death I guess, is what that bottle makes me think of. Gulp and wince. Rush toward death with numbness in your toes. Maybe my brother-in-law will come back saying that the earth below us is underwater. But the radio says things are better and that signal has to come from somewhere. The classics can't hold my attention. My brain skitters and starts. I hear my nephews running downstairs. I feel the pull towards holding my baby, smoothing her hair, saying Mama's sorry for shooting that deer. Guilt like an ice pick down my esophagus. Breathe in and out. Like those apps said when we were lulled into thinking things would calm down if we tried hard enough to calm ourselves. The binders. My uncle's multi-colored plastic binders. They'll never biodegrade. I used to wish that a scientist would invent a new strain of bacteria that could eat plastic. Eat plastic and burp out flowers. Now, I bet we've lost all of the people who could do that. All of the people who could farm. All of the people who could study germs. Now, I bet, we're a mouldering circus of writers and actors and semi-pro baseball players, befuddled at the thought of killing our own food. Flipping through the binders, I see the investments. Most of it doesn't make sense to me, but every once in a while, a word. Oxycontin. Distribution. Things like that. The unshakable foundation of houses like this, high on a mountain, safe from everything else. My uncle's money like long fangs biting into the world below, sucking, sucking, but now it's started to rain. Out the window, I see that it's raining and that makes me happy. I don't know why, but my thoughts have been so dry lately. I hope that another deer adopted the orphaned baby. I hope I don't go down as a legend to the deer. The two-legged monster with a loud bang. I hope we don't invent violence all over again, but this time bigger and better and more. I read through my uncle's binders, fingers skimming over the numbers. So much money, none of it tangible, flowing in, in, in, in. And now he's dead. Remember when your mother died? You weren't there, but I thought her body was the first dead person I'd ever seen that looked alive. Like she could be sleeping. Like she was happy to finally be dead. Overhead, thunder claps, and I think it serves us right. I put down the binders. The money. My uncle died of heart failure. Not even in his mountain house. He was in the back of a town car talking on his cell phone. Making plans for dinner, we never found out who with. He keeled over and died before any of this happened. And now we're in his fortress and I'm glad and I'm sorry. I go downstairs because my baby doesn't like thunder. It's too loud and confusing. The dogs have their ears down, their tails down. I take my baby in my lap on the sofa and kiss her head like I imagined doing. She smells clean like I imagined. Outside, the rain falls in sheets. Washing water down the mountain. Down, down, down.

MEGAN LOOKS ASKANCE AT THE GIRL WITH the multi-colored markers, Polly. Polly used to pop bubblegum, but there's no more bubblegum in the world. I could have told you, pills, distribution, bad, bad things. How does a man make enough money to build a house on a mountain? Through kindness? Through generosity? Megan wants to know if I'm okay with Polly being here and I say sure even though I can smell the rotting flesh of a beached whale on the air. Maybe that's just the wind shifting from the burned out bar. Maybe it's just the charbroiled congregation. We have to dig up the nonperishables. Megan helps me. Dog watches. Polly sits in the car. I buried enough cans in the sand to last me ten years. I never thought I'd get up again, move somewhere else, tumble on. I was ready to stick to the desert, but it's hard to put down roots in the sand, and anyway, Megan's eyes are wild and I don't like the way she's stopped talking about the future. We dig for a long time before we hit the cans and when we do, Megan laughs like we're pirates who've struck gold. We're covered in sweat and sand and then there's Polly at the lip of our nonperishable pit saying she brought beers and Megan smiles at me, the exercise working loose the suspicion in her muscles. We sprawl, cans half-loaded into the truck, and drink our beers. I still tell my body to get drunk, but it won't. Megan wants to know the things that Polly knows about me. What was I like when I was younger? Polly smiles her mean smile. She was scared, is what she says, although that's not quite right, or at least, that's not all of it. I was scared of the small power in my hands. We'll bring Giles when we go. He'll live for a long long time. I think we're going to invent violence again. I don't think there's any way around that. It's going to be worse than it was, and I've got such a meager antidote. I don't believe you, Megan says, she's not afraid of anything. I can feel pride shining out of my eyes because that's who I've always wanted to be. A tough broad who isn't afraid of anything. I slit that rabbit open after you chickened out and I convinced myself to do it by telling myself I wasn't afraid. And then what did I read in the blood and entrails? Fear fear fear. It's been trailing me my whole life, shaped like a rabbit, or else shaped like my father's face contorted with rage. She's afraid of high tide, Polly says, and that's true. I'm afraid of the deep things high tide brings to the surface. Well, there's no tide here, Megan says. We dance around talking about the city, or the outskirts, or some town. We're afraid that if we mention it, if we call it into being, then it'll come in the night and take our cans away. We could eat out of the truck for years. I wonder if that's why Polly is here. For the food. You think that the radio's lying? Megan is looking down at her beer, peeling the label from its sweaty surface. I think maybe I shouldn't let her drink so much. Maybe whatever grasping need took her mother lives in Megan too. It's lying a little bit, Polly says, looking up at the sky. Half of her legs are completely covered in sand. She looks like she sprung cactus-like from the ground. But that doesn't mean none of it's true. I take a long swig of my beer and try to tell my body to get drunk, to get soft, to give in. But, I'm on high alert since Polly came back. Her body like a knife stuck in a tree trunk. Danger. Fear fear fear. I'm about to open my mouth to speak when, impossible, improbable, how can it be? But it is, a low rumble of thunder unfurls itself overhead.

My brother-in-law comes back, soaked to the bone. He's grinning and, at first, that makes me afraid because I think he's seen what he wanted to see at the bottom of the mountain. Desolation. Despair. But, no. He's grinning because he saw green shoots. He saw life. He said, the air is so clear. He said, the water shines like a mirror. You could see your face in it, he says. His dourness is gone. His frown. The man who pressed his ear to the late night radio and waited for the doom he felt in his heart to be confirmed is gone. In his place is a sunflower of a man. It's true, he says, the radio isn't lying. I pull my baby close to me. She's gotten bigger since we've been here. Every little change is bigger in babies. I wondered if we could just stay up here until she was big and strong. Grown. Then, she could handle whatever was at the bottom of the mountain. There aren't enough apologies in the world for me to make to my baby about what's waiting out there. How do you know?—my sister asks. Now she's the skeptical one. She wanted her husband to come back grinning, but now that he is, wet and cold and smiling from ear to ear, she doesn't trust it. She can't quite believe it because it's what she wants and when in this life does a man come through the door and tell you exactly what you want to hear? I ran into a family driving an RV, my brother in law says. There's still gas?—my mother asks. Behind and around us, the boys are zooming. All they heard was their father's happiness. His assurance that everything has returned to normal. There must still be some gas, my brother-in-law says because this family was driving the RV. They were all wearing overalls, he says. And?—my sister wants to know, her brows arched in utmost skepticism. They were wearing overalls, so what? So, the apocalypse didn't happen after all. No, no, my brother-in-law says. It happened. There are dead people and burned out buildings and overgrown shopping centers everywhere. Someone burned down the kayak rental stand. There was a skeleton behind the counter. White skull. Keep your voice down, my sister says. The boys didn't hear, although they'd love to go see a white skull renting kayaks. But, it's over now. It's over? Well, the weather isn't over, that part isn't over, but it's amazing how, with fewer people, you know, alive, everything is cleaner. The air. The grass. The trees. The rocks. Rocks can't be cleaner, my sister says, but my brother-in-law ignores her. He's on a roll. They say there's no more bullets. They say there's enough food for everyone. People are driving back to the cities, rebuilding buildings, regrowing gardens. How many people?—I ask. My brother-in-law turns to me and frowns. I don't know, he says. But I do. Hardly any. Just us in our mountain house. Ill gotten. And that family in their RV. The people who got out of the city when they had the chance. The people with luck and somewhere to go. So, you think we should pack up here?—my mother asks. We all turn our eyes to my brother-in-law. We're all hoping he'll say what he says: I'm saying we can go home.

NO WAY, MEGAN MURMURS AS THE THUNDER gets louder. I think of their dead bodies. All the dead bodies. Too many humans and now we're mostly dead and since we're mostly dead the air is cleaner and the rain comes. We better get inside, Polly says, not liking the lightning flash on the horizon. It looks god-thrown. Megan has her mouth open, daring the rain to fall. We can't, I say, but I can't explain why. I lived with Polly by the ocean. We had nothing but water. But here, this, the preacher-man cowering behind the bar.

The congregation, sticky blue-mouthed. No way, Megan says again. Hasn't it rained?–Polly asks–her voice panic-high. It reminds me of a cresting wave. No, I say. It hasn't rained. And just then, the first few drops fall, and then we're out in it. Out in a downpour that rolls off the compact surface of the sand. What life is left runs to take shelter, but Megan, her fists balled up in rage at her sides, runs, gangly, out into the desert. Her fleeing silhouette puts me in mind of the girl that first showed up to my trailer, wanting to know the future. I wouldn't have told her that it was going to rain. Dog takes off after Megan, but Polly and I stop and stare, drenched. Shouldn't we move?–Polly screams, but it's hard to hear her over the rain. It's up to my ankles. Flash flood. I'm watching Megan fleeing and I'm telling myself to move my feet, but I can see a motorcycle in my head, an impulse, a leather jacket. It doesn't rain here, I say, but too quietly for Polly to hear. Dog circles back around and looks at me, so I follow him into the desert rain. There's almost no wind. The sky is burnt-orange. Behind me, Polly takes refuge in her truck. I can hear her thoughts, hear her call me crazy or lovesick. But Megan is my family now. Megan and Dog and the trailer. Why does the weather change? Why does the rain come? Megan is a damp spot on the horizon. It's dangerous!–I yell at her. It's dangerous to be the tallest thing on the ground during a lightning storm. The lightning is purple and orange and white overhead. Megan is the tallest thing. There aren't any more tall cacti raising their hands towards the sun. I think of Megan's man, then, and his red-haired waitress. I think of how she wouldn't be here now, in the rain, if he'd just taken her with him. Desire, fickle. Megan, stop!–I yell and her body goes still on the horizon. It will take me a minute to catch up with her. Walking in wet sand is hard on my legs. But I will walk. I will not turn around. I will not climb into Polly's warm truck and watch the rain as if it were happening to someone, somewhere, else. Hold up, hold up, I tell myself. Don't go anywhere.

So now it is all packing, explaining, hoping, doing laundry. How do we get all the nonperishables in the car? The baby looks at me, alive, alive, we're all still alive. All still alive and healthy. No tetanus shots needed. No rabies shots. Nothing we can't get. I think of the pharmacy at the end of my city block. The one that didn't take my insurance. Right at the start, those windows were smashed in. People taking pills and injections they needed or wanted and couldn't get before. The kind of giddy euphoria of collapse. Everything is free now! We are free now? I'm folding our sweaters, our jeans, my hands shaking. Are we going home?—I ask my husband. Sort of, he says. But I know we won't be going back to my kitchen, my bathroom, my sofa. I know that the city burned. We could see the flames as we drove to the mountain. I know that the streets are empty now. That the pills and injections were long sold to those who could afford them—no longer free. We'll all go back to my mom and dad's house. Back to the place where we were raised. Our cul de sac. Remember the woods? Remember how we felt like it was a wilderness. How we, children, didn't understand that we, children, were the most dangerous things in those woods? Still are. Still will be. My parents' neighborhood didn't burn. We expect a wall.

A wall with a familiar face at the helm who will welcome us in. Who will believe we are who we say we are. Who will let us keep our cans of food. And, I should feel guilty, the broken neck of the mama deer, but I feel my mouth water at the prospect of a garden. Why didn't you wait for me? We could grow our own food. Melons, tomatoes, potatoes, cucumbers, basil. Basil will grow anywhere, breathing in and out in the humid air. I bet they have medicine. One of our neighbors was a doctor at the most famous hospital in the world. If you'd waited for me instead of running away, we could have lived through this together. You could be coming back with us to my parents' house. To the wall we were born behind. I bet the soil will be saved. And, I'm thinking about all the things we might have—a generator? A clear stream? Remember the stream? Remember our adolescent pagan rites? That the cabin around me begins to fade. Turn to ash. This is nothing. This, alone on the mountain, surrounded by a paved trail, surrounded by deer and trees. This is not a community. This isolation. We will drive home. Drive home. Like we used to. My heart can't fathom how there is still gasoline. Outside, the rain soaks into the green. I hope it is raining wherever you are.

I CAN'T BELIEVE YOU'RE GOING HOME. GOING back. I reach Megan in the rain and Dog is circling, howling, his tail between his legs. What are you doing?–I shout, but it's no use. Around us, the storm roars. It's like being inside a seashell. I know that a seashell's noise is just blood rushing inside a brain. It's like that. A roar of blood circulating. Megan's mouth is open, her pink tongue extended. Water everywhere. Maybe this is how I die? Drowned upright in the desert. Megan is screaming, or at least her neck is bulging like she's screaming, but I can't hear the sound. Dog is determined not to leave her side even as the rain comes harder, feels like slaps. Our skin pinks. I remember our cul de sac. What I wouldn't give for a wall. I can't make Megan hear me, so I grab her wrist. She stares at me then. Stops screaming for a moment. I pull her wrist to say: Here. Stay here. Stay on this ground with me. She nods. Laces her fingers in mine. Tugs at my hand to say: scream. Scream now. Get it out. So we do. We raise our heads and we scream and scream until a bolt of lightning strikes the sand near us. A fizz over the ground. Dog leaps into the air. We fall, still holding hands. Dizzy, but not electrified. And then, for a moment, time slows and warps. I waited for you instead of stealing the motorcycle. I waited for you and your parents took me in and now we're sisters, closer than sisters, and I'm entitled to that wall, that garden, that medicine. I'm like you. But, when my mind clears, all I'm holding is Megan and Dog and the rain. We stand and the thing in Megan snaps so she can run and we run back to the trailer. The whole way my legs ache. A leftover tingle from the lightning. Like biting into something soft and cold. Shivers. We ignore Polly in her truck, but I can feel her eyes on us. She's used to seeing me in water. The sea. How I thought I'd always live by the sea and even when I tried to get away from it, the sea found me here. The early flood warnings were so loud. So loud, and so useless. Everything got washed away. We slam the door of the trailer, me and Megan and Dog. Dog looks so happy. He's grinning a wide Dog grin and dancing from paw to paw. When he shakes water all over us, we don't even scold him. Megan has her hands on her knees, panting at the floor. I can't believe it fucking rained, she says. It's raining, I say. But you'll still come with me? And Polly? We can ditch Polly, I say, quick, in case she thinks my loyalties are divided. But you'll still leave? Of course, Megan says, but she doesn't look up at me. Her hair hangs limp over her face. Her braids unbraided. The rain pounds on the trailer's metal roof and she won't meet my eyes.

This night might be the last night. One of the last on the mountain. I can't sleep. Have had a hard time sleeping since the deer. Since I shot the deer dead. My baby looks grown to me now, and still so fragile. My husband smiles a little. He's thinking of all the neighbors my parents had that are dead now. The generators, the food, the clothes the blankets the silver the gold. I imagine myself running my hands through other women's jewelry boxes. I don't deserve it, but they didn't deserve it either. Nobody deserves jewels. We can move in next door, my husband says, killing off my parents' nearest neighbor. An elderly couple I've known all my life. We can move in there and your parents can be in their house with your sister and the boys and we'll have a family commune thing, he says. Like the Kennedeys, he says. I think of the people who will be left. Not the best of us, surely. Not those who tried to help. And the food. There was a neighbor with a bunker. An old man with a camo-colored fishing hat who told us the Mormons were going to survive the apocalypse. They have cellars, he told us. I bet you're alive. Out of everyone, I bet you made it. I think it's the gold power in your hands. Can you even die? Or will you go on forever, disapproving of me and my safe choices? Or, maybe you don't disapprove, maybe you understand, I bet that's it. Like how you wanted to pretend to be drunk, even though you were never convincing. After you ran away, I went to college with a hard shell around me. There's no one here to fix you now. That's what I told myself. You were gone, so all of my bruises would actually bruise. All of my wounds would leave scars. Once I found my husband, it was something like the safety of a friend who can bring back a dead squirrel. But, no special powers here. We're going back to where I was born. My baby will run in the same woods, wilder. I hear a noise outside. Shuffling, like footsteps.

A human cough. I go rigid in the bed, but my husband is asleep. His body is loose. I wonder if he's dreaming of cans of beans, Mormon-esque cellars, safety, safety, safety. My baby is asleep too, I can hear her deep breath. In and out. In and out. This is the air that will make her body whole. This is the environment that will shape her. I don't get up. There is no more gun now. I don't go to the kitchen in search of a knife. I think, if it's him, if it's the outsideman, I'll let him crawl through the window, his shaggy beard trailing like fog, and I'll let him kill me. I wait in the night, but the footsteps move on. The shadow doesn't linger.

I WAKE WITH A START IN THE NIGHT. NOT because of your insomniac voice. I hear your voice all the time, a low murmur, and it doesn't keep me awake. If I don't focus, I don't hear the individual words. I just hear that you're alive and your family is alive, so the place that gave birth to me and raised me, the first love I ever had, is alive. No, I'm awake because there was a scream. I look and Megan and Dog are gone. The fear is cold as it falls through my body. I don't even bother with shoes. Let the scorpions return. Let them try to poison me. Outside is so black. Night black, forever black. Then, a faint light, a flashlight. Out in the desert where I buried the cans. Another scream. A whistle. I run. Dog barks. He hops helplessly between them, Megan and Polly. Megan has her shovel raised high in the air. Polly is covered in sand. The hole at their feet is deep enough to be a grave. She was trying to take the food, Megan says, voice hard and gritty. No I wasn't, Polly says, but I know she was. I know, like lightning, that that's why she's here. She was never good at planning, but she is good at stealing.

Put the shovel down, I say, but Megan ignores me. She was going to put all of the cans we had left here into her truck. You're crazy, Polly says. Hearing her say that, I'm back at the beach, colored markers inking the inside of my wrists. A dead whale. Something rotten that attracts all sorts of creatures. Polly's teeth are white in the dark. I'm not crazy. You're the preacher-man, Megan says. Her eyes do look crazy. Wild. But she's got a good reason. You're the preacher man hiding behind the bar while everyone dies. What the fuck are you talking about?—Polly asks, throws her hands up in a dramatic gesture. Maybe it's the gesture that bothers Megan, she swings the shovel down. There's still water, unabsorbed on the ground. The sand is like tar, grasping at our ankles. Everything is stickier and tougher than it would otherwise be. If there were scorpions, they've drowned. And, in this moment, I want to come with you. Back to the cul-de-sac. Back to my parents' house on the other side of the street. You can move in there, move your baby into my old bedroom. Raise her up to question things and to fight. Polly dodges the shovel easily. You're a crazy person!—she shouts at Megan, who is panting, sweating, at the end of her rope. Everybody calm down, I say, I raise my hands, but they ignore me, even as Dog looks my way. Polly and Megan have their hackles up, at the lip of the pit. The hard cans, what we haven't moved to my car, glint at the bottom like rocks in a riverbed. I'm not crazy, Megan says. She swings the shovel again, Polly dodges again. They grunt like female tennis stars. People like you think nobody else is real! You don't care if the rest of us die. On *die,* Megan swings her hardest. She misses by a mile, but the force of it twists her ankle and I watch the shadow of her stagger, tip, and fall into the pit. There is a dull thud in the desert. Stupid bitch, Polly says. Dog whines. Then, the black night is silent.

In the morning it's: make a list, make a plan, double check. My sister's face is stretched into a grin. So is my mother's. They're no longer low level fighting without words. No more psychic laser beams. They are moving as one, a being with many arms and legs, packing boxes, packing suitcases, checking things off of lists. The boys are hiding from their mother because they don't want to leave the forest. They're the little kings of the forest. They don't understand what it means to go home. To hole up. To sit behind a wall with other people, safe. The dogs smell something on the air too. They're whining, their nails click click in circles on the floor. The cat is aloof. Her life is the same no matter where we take her. She hates the indignity of her travel box but once she's out, she's a queen again. Are we doing this?—my sister keeps asking herself. She whispers it, all in one breath, whoosh, are we doing this? Are we packing up and driving down the mountain? We can admit that we never thought we'd drive down. Now that the possibility of forever atop the mountain has crumbled before us, we can tell each other that we were afraid to be the last humans on earth. That we thought the children would see the concrete wood path crumble and return to nature. That our children's (incestuous) children would know how to butcher deer. We laugh, quick out breaths, ha ha, and touch our knees, bellies, lower backs. Vulnerable places. It's my job to put the cans in the car. Nonperishables.

It's important that we bring all the food. Even the food that the boys think is disgusting—canned olives, canned sardines. It will all come in handy. I wonder if I've absorbed all of the metals of the can these past few months. If I am now, at least part can. Sturdy. Metallic. My mother and sister frown at me as I move from pantry to car, pantry to car. They are sure I'm doing something wrong, but they're not sure what it is. Above and around and through us, the radio plays its jubilee. Come home, the radio says. It's safe enough. Return, return, return. It's playing songs from my girlhood. Songs from summer bar-be-ques, songs from Preakness parties, songs from crab feasts. Dancing in the moonlight. Remember dogwood trees? Remember our parents, drunk and dancing, making fools out of themselves in their forties? I remember thinking with such disgusted precision, that I would never be like that. Now, I know I won't, but just because we might run out of booze in ten years. Although, the neighborhood must have a still or two in the works. Some enterprising dads. Come back to where you were born, the radio tells me. And all I can think of is you, the witch girl next door, my very first friend. I hope you're not dead. Who will my baby have to grow up and get hurt with? Who will run the woods with her while her cousins brandish their sharp sticks and tell her that the woods belong to girls? My husband puts his hand on my back. Hey, he says, gentle. He's been gentle since (oh god) the deer. You okay? Yeah, I say, frowning at the rows and rows of canned beans in the car. Just thinking. Me too, he says, and I know he sees my parents' home as a building project. Rebuild. Replace. Renew. He will tear down the creeping green vines that connect your window to mine.

OH GOD, OH GOD, OH GOD. HE COMES BACK
to me in flashes, that dead God on a cross. Blood. There's
blood at Megan's temple. Polly is stepping back, her palms
up, saying I didn't do anything, I didn't touch her. I jump
into the pit. It's a hard pit. Cans. You're frowning at cans. I'm
frowning at cans. Megan's head is bleeding. Oh God, I don't

want to touch her. I don't want to realize there's nothing I can do. It wasn't even that steep! Polly is crying, and I know she didn't mean it, but I want to call a lightning bolt from the sky. Shut up, I hiss. I move Megan's head towards me. Her eyes roll behind her eyelids. Her skin is still warm. She's still breathing. Maybe she just knocked herself out. You just wanted the fucking food?—I ask and I think I'm quiet enough that Polly doesn't hear, but she does. Yeah, she said, I figured you had some. You always had some for other people. I wasn't going to take it all. Help me, I say, and Polly, astonishingly, does. We take Megan back to the trailer and lay her down on the futon. Dog lies at her feet and whines, big brown Dog eyes pleading with me to do something. It's nice in here, Polly says and it's all I can do not to turn on her and say shut up, shut up, shut up. I'm sorry, she says again, after minutes of me sitting, in silence beside Megan. Who is still breathing. But who knows if that purple splotch at her temple is bleeding under the skin. Who knows what the corner of a can of beans is doing to her brain. Polly can say sorry all she wants. It rushes past me like the ocean. Megan wanted me to read her cards. Read her future. I saw purple on her, purple like her brother's dead feet. Purple like her mother's dead face. Now this, this purple spreading from her temple to the rest of her. This purple bruise, this purple death, this purple fall. She's your new girlfriend? Impossible, but Polly is still in the trailer, still talking to me. She has a marker in her hand, lime green. She's my family, I say. Polly nods. That's nice. I've got nobody. As if this is the time to tell me about her own problems. It wouldn't occur to Polly that her malice is why she's alone. I've got nobody because I've been

170

waiting for you, she says. Shut up, I say, finally, it escapes my lips. Dog perks his ears at me, surprised. Can I draw something? Can I draw something on you?—Polly asks and I stick out my arm so she'll stop talking. I can feel the felt tip of her marker over my veins. I want the ink inside me. I want to be green and cool like a tropical plant. I want Megan's purple bruise to disappear. Polly draws a watermelon. There aren't any more watermelons, and now I can only remember what the fake version tasted like. Laffy Taffy. Starburst. Lip Smackers. Megan is breathing regularly, her eyes rolling, but she doesn't wake. If she doesn't wake soon, she won't wake at all. The light pulses in my fingers. Giles looks at me from the terrarium on the kitchen table. The thing is, I know I could fix her, if I wanted to, if I tried, but I'm not sure what it'd do to me. Like my mother. I almost died. This, how much closer is this—Megan's limbs akimbo, her skin pale—to death than my mother was? It's a watermelon, Polly says, as if I couldn't feel it taking shape. When was the last time you saw a watermelon?—she's saying it to herself, so I don't answer. I can feel in every stroke of that marker that she wanted to come collect me and my food and bundle me away. That she wasn't counting on Megan, or Dog even. I feel Giles' ancient gecko eyes on me. I feel the light in the palm of my hand.

Once the cars are packed, a hesitance settles over us. The boys drag their feet and declare everything stupid. The dogs huddle together and whine. The sun is setting, so we decide that we should leave in the morning. In the dawn of a new day. I feel the uncertainty gnawing at me reflected in everyone's faces. Now that it's come down to it, now that the radio's chirping voice has been switched off, we're not sure we should go after all. How easy would it be to unload everything and keep existing as we have been. We're better off than some people. We have safety. We have food. People, mostly, leave us alone. The outsideman's face flickers in my mind. I think of the deer. The gun has no more bullets, but that doesn't mean I couldn't use a knife, a rock, my hands. I start to tremble. Where has this violence come from? Spilling over from the top of me. I can barely catch it as it falls. My husband and I take the baby on a final walk. We want to put distance between ourselves and the rest of the family, even if the idea of a nuclear family has exploded with the rest of the world. A final walk on the concrete ring. My baby looks at me like a wise nun. She's grown so much in these months. In her, I see all of the changes we've undergone. Everything that has grown and changed and died and regrown. In the woods, my husband holds my hand. He wants to soothe me because he can see the violence trembling under my skin. It'll be okay, he says. What about the drive?–I ask because I want to ask about logistics and not about the thing that is worrying my mind. What do you mean? I mean are there bandits on the road? Are the roads still passable? I don't know, he says. It's not that far of a drive. On our drive out here, early in the gray morning, I tried not to think. Everyone was so tired. Now, we are brimming with nervous energy, eager to get on the road, eager to get back. Then how do you know it'll be alright?–I ask him. I know it's not a fair question, no one knows anything. Remember when we were girls? Remember the woods and our sincere belief in your magic? I knowit was real, all of it. I believe you have a power inside of you that no one else has. That you are the real thing. It'll be okay as long as we're together, my husband says, and a swoop of love brushes its feather inside me. I guess he's right. As long as we can cling together with whatever unearned favors we've been granted by circumstance, then we should be all right. Ahead of us, dusk falls on the concrete loop. I squint to see a shadow. I think I hear rustling footsteps. But, we keep moving. The three of us. A family. Into the dark.

YOU COULD DO SOMETHING ABOUT THIS, Polly says, gesturing towards Megan as the night grows darker around us. I feel it in my body, a humming light. I see, not the trailer, not Dog, not Polly or Giles in his little glass world, but the blue faces of the congregation, one after the other, splayed where they landed after slumping to the barroom floor. I know, I say. I'm waiting to see if she'll wake up. You can wake her up, Polly says, as if she doesn't know the consequences. She knows. She saw me, at the beach, revive a cat in an alley once. I've always had a soft spot for cats. Remember that tailless calico in our neighborhood? I used to pretend she was a girl transformed. A girl who transformed herself so she could live outside and kill her own food. Polly saw me revive a miserable alley cat once, it was foolish, a waste of energy, but I couldn't stand to see its broken body. It looked like it'd gotten in a fight with a dog. Polly dragged me out back to kiss me in the dark. Oh bars. The smokey laughter that disappears when you open and close a door in the night? She kissed me with too much teeth, but I liked the sharpness of it, and then there was this broken cat's body over her shoulder. I knelt before I thought too deeply about it. I brought the light to the cat and it revived, stretched, meowed at me, green eyes like alien moons, and then it slinked away. Polly stared. I felt her lipstick on my mouth. Orange. I didn't know you could do that, she said, eyes narrowed. I braced myself for my father's fear. Rage red face. But Polly smiled. Are you a witch?–she asked, pulling me closer. Are you green underneath your skin? I let her bite my neck, my earlobe, in the dark. I thought about that cat for a long time. I hope it didn't get run over the next day. What's the point in saving a cat?–Polly asked. You can save a person now, you can save your family, now. But Polly knew, she knew that I stumbledlike a drunk for the rest of the night after the cat slunk away. She knew that my body caved in on itself, empty of energy. And that was just a cat. Imagine Megan's body, a full woman's body, imagine all of the energy it would suck from my hands. Would there be anything left?

Polly was saying the same thing she always said: wouldn't it be fun, exciting, sexy, if you hurt yourself? Wouldn't your pain be something to admire? Megan shifted on the futon and I put my hand on her forehead. I could feel the light leaping up, wanting to be used. I'll look after her, Polly said, her face half-obscured by the coming night. She meant she'd take Megan and the food with her, if I died.

We see nothing in the woods and we make it back safe. And I'm thinking about how unfair our safety is, even if, baby strapped to my chest, I don't want anything to happen to us, ever. I haven't seen the outsideman since I shot the deer. I wonder how long it takes a deer to rot in the woods, to become a skeleton. Is she a skeleton now? No, it's too soon. The dogs are pacing, the cat rubs her orange face against my ankles. The animals know that, in the morning, we're moving. We leave the place clean. My sister even scrubbed the toilets. Like it's a vacation rental and we'll be charged for our mess. I think of lighting all of my uncle's papers on fire in the front yard, cleanse it spiritually, but I don't have the skills to keep a fire under control. I'd burn everything down by accident. Remember the schoolgirl outfits? What was the biggest decision we made in those woods? Whether or not to believe in magic. You did and I didn't and I knew it even then. My baby, my girl, looks at me with her new old-person eyes and I kiss her head and I tell her I'm sorry. I'm going to become productive when we go back behind the wall. I'm going to learn to can food for the winter, to preserve, to grow, to kill chickens, on purpose, not deer in a fit of fear in

175

the night. My mother turns on the radio. It's playing music. When was the last time the radio played music? I let my girl out of the baby holder and she wobbles on her chubby feet, but she's stronger now than she was when we first arrived. My husband bends and dances with her. My brother-in-law dances with my mother. My sister takes my hand and spins me. We dance like we're children, clumsy, like we've forgotten what dancing is for. Remember the woods? Remember the music and our young bodies? I chafed at being called young then, I thought it was synonymous with unserious, and I wanted nothing more than to be serious and adult. Now, I'd do anything to be a child again, running in the woods, before all this, oblivious that all this waited behind a hill. Catastrophe. We brought it upon ourselves. Too late, I feel bad. Too late, I realize my inadequacies. Remember dancing under the moon, its round face reflected in the lake water? Remember how, almost, there was real magic between us? My father is smoking weed in the garage. The music on the radio is a tune from our childhood. Upbeat, drums, You Make Me Dizzy Miss Lizzy. Dance, dance, dance. Remember when we played music from our phones by the lake and I kissed that blonde boy in all innocence and you never once, not ever, got drunk? There is a frantic sort of happiness jumping around behind everyone's skin. Tomorrow, we drive down the mountain to see what we can see. Tomorrow we will face destruction and the terrible fact of our own survival. But tonight the radio plays music, and we dance.

AND WHAT CHOICE DO I HAVE? I HEAR YOU, I hear that you're moving down the mountain, back to the woods and the walls and the songs of our childhood. Do I remember the lake? The lake leaps up at me, the pulsing soundtrack of our high school years, so uncool to me now. Leaps up in vivid detail as the light and the energy builds up in my hands. Megan isn't going to wake up on her own, I will have to wake her. And in my heart, there is peace alongside the fear. Peace that this, at least, is something good I can do. Dog whines. I remember the rabbit. The rabbit that I killed just to learn that I could, just to learn that blood didn't scare me, just to learn that, for a certain form of life, fear is all there is. I'll take care of her, Polly says, but I don't even hear Polly. I see her yellow suitcase moving into the beach house. I see how blue her hair was then. I feel my old leather jacket on my shoulders. I swear I smell it. Is this what it's like to die? To be flooded with your life memories? To have your life enter you and overflow your body with detail and sensation. How quickly I skip over my father's red-rage face, how long I linger on an afternoon in the desert, hot, hot, Megan on the futon, Dog snoring. How long each of his Dog breaths are. Is that profound? I feel a lot of pressure to think something profound as I die, to have you finally hear me. When we slit our palms with safety scissors, you said they weren't supposed to be able to hurt us, and I laughed, and I put our blood together because when you're young *forever* doesn't seem real. I didn't think through the logistics of having your voice in my head for the rest of my life, but, honestly, it's kept me from loneliness in dark times. It's kept me from despair. If you could hear me, I'd say thank you, I'll say it anyway. Thank you. All the light rushes out of me and it tastes like lake water. It sounds like the tinny speakers on a phone, it feels like sitting on the ground trying to be drunk. Life, life, life, it feels, in its small way, like every grain of sand living inside me opens a small sand mouth and sings a high pure note. Symphony of life. I put my hands on Megan's chest, over her heart, because that's where doctors put the paddles to shock you back to life. Listen, listen, listen, I don't have much inside of me, but you can have it. *Forever.* Be long lived, see the cities come back, try harder, do better, next time.

Our suitcases are packed in the blue morning. Now that it's come to it, we're quiet. The dancing euphoria of last night's party has worn off and we're afraid. Dangerous thoughts creep over us. There could be people on the road with weapons. Just because we've heard that all the bullets ran out, doesn't mean they haven't started melting things down to make more. I almost wish my husband hadn't shot the last of ours into the ground. Deer skull. I'm sorry. My baby doesn't fuss. The dogs don't howl. Even the boys, long affronted by the idea of leaving their wooded kingdom, are subdued. They know that this is a journey back. They are the ones who will have to grow up, claw back, and it's not fair, and I hope they don't become bitter because of it. If they do, they'll repeat our harms. Warm brown deer eyes, flashing in the dark. My sister thinks about locking the door, but then doesn't. She puts the key in the mailbox. The town is burned out, the town people are dead, but maybe the raccoons and the deer and the hawks and the songbirds will wander in. Maybe they'll clutch coffee cups in their talons and look out of the glass door in the morning, marveling at the trees. Wind moves through tree branches in the blue morning, and it's cleaner and brighter than it ever was in the city, and when we go back, we don't know what we'll find. Everybody buckled up?—my husband asks, like we're going on a family trip to the zoo. The normalcy of his voice startles me. The cat meows from her travel carrier, annoyed with us all. Our car's snout is pointed bravely down the driveway. My husband has his back to the cabin, to the wood and metal and glass that we are leaving to rot. To be reclaimed. I twist in the passenger's seat to check on my baby one last time. To make sure that her car seat is secure. She smiles at me and I feel my heart fill up with love. For one beat, there is no fear. Then, behind us, in the window of my uncle's office, I see a face. I freeze. It's the outsideman, beard wild, eyes wide, face gaunt. He's watching us from the office. Wasn't I just in the office? He puts his palm flat against the windowpane. A warning. How long has he been in the house? Maybe he never left.

You okay?—my husband asks and I turn around quickly. Remember when you thought you could hear my voice in your head? And you tried and tried to shout my name without words, but I never heard you? When your mother died, I shouted your name, but I heard nothing back. I feel the outsideman's eyes on my neck. He's not doing anything besides watching us go. He will reclaim the cabin once we're gone.

I want to say, I've always felt like you were reading my thoughts. In the quiet, before it's all family and pets and road. I want to say I'm sorry. I'm sorry for how casual I was with your heart. Like a heart isn't something that can stop at any time. Like we're not all just one catastrophe away from death. I am sorry. I should have sent you something in the mail. I should have followed you. I feel like you've been carrying me this whole time, and now, pulling away from the cabin and the outsideman and the trees and the deer, I think I see you again, crouching over something, your face older but twisted in a familiar look of concentration. You're at peace. But you're afraid. Do you need me? I'm here, reaching out, light on wild light—do you remember when? Safety scissors. Rabbit. Blood. Stones. Moss. Fighting with sticks in our parents' yards. Don't give up now. Keep fighting. Here is my light for you. I scream your name. I hear you calling. Can you hear me? I remember.

You okay?—my husband asks. Yeah fine, all strapped in, I say, and one by one, mother, father, sister, us. We rev our engines and roll down the mountain.

I HEARD YOU AFTER MY MOTHER DIED. I HEARD you scream my name. I felt you with me over Megan's body, encircling us with a light that eats itself and dies and returns and lives. I felt your spark add itself to mine, and it was enough. It was enough to fill me up and to bring Megan back. For that, I thank you. For once, I'm not exhausted. Do you even know what you can do?

Megan, Dog, and I are taking the trailer and we're heading back to the place I know you'll go. To where my father's crumbling house is. To our father's backyards. I'm bringing a hammer, I'm bringing some nails and sandpaper too. It's the one place I can think of, the one place that might take us all in, and Megan likes that it's not in the middle of a city. She, a desert girl, never lived anywhere with more than three stop lights. Polly isn't coming. Not because she doesn't want to. She'd follow us and suck our energy and take tiny bites of our love to eat for as long as we let her, but no, we told her, you can't come. Not this time. I gave her some food, though. She didn't fight me on it. When Megan woke up under my hands, I was sure that I was dead. I've read that your brain can still focus for a few minutes after you die. I wondered if it was a gift, getting to see her open her eyes, getting to see her smile at me in wonder. But, no, the light in me had not extinguished, it multiplied. I didn't feel weak, I felt strong. Such a simple magic. True love's kiss. That's when I told Polly to go and she did, seeing the golden light underneath my skin. I expected a parting shot, something nasty, flung to fester, but instead she was quiet. Thoughtful. I didn't feel as triumphant as I thought I would. I felt like I was watching the sun set behind the body of a whale. She drove away and pulled up her tethers, releasing me, finally, from doubt and guilt and shame. So, I tell Megan, we'll head to my father's house. It's a white house with green shutters and a black door. Who paints their door black?—Megan wants to know. She says she'll try to get her hands on some paint. Try to paint the door red or blue or yellow. I have a friend who lives next door, I tell her. A friend from when I was a child. From when it was easy and natural to make friends.

The purple bruise on Megan's forehead fades before my eyes. Dog licks her face. We pack the food and Megan peppers me with questions. How many bedrooms does my father's house have? How do I know that it's safe? I don't know, I tell her, it's just a feeling. A hope. I have a friend there. So, then she wants to know about you. I tell her about when we were schoolgirls, I tell her about the schoolgirl outfits. She says, that sounds nice. She says, growing up, my brother was my only friend. So, our last stop out of town is the graveyard. A solemn place all stone and sand and dust. A monument to a town that has nothing left to speak for it. Megan kneels and touches her brother's name. It reminds me of my mother's grave, of my mother's small magic. She whispers something I don't hear to the stone, then turns to me. Does it rain where we're going?—she asks. Yes, I say. It rains. So we go.

ACKNOWLEDGMENTS

This novella is a dream come true. Thank you to Leslie Jill Patterson for judging the Clay Reynolds Novella Prize and for choosing my manuscript.

Thank you to the entire team at the TRP for your hard work and dedication, especially PJ Carlisle who is a patient and brilliant editor.

Thank you to my family: Mom, Dad, Molly, Brian, and Joe. Thank you for your love and support.

Thank you to Nancy Nguyen and Aleyna Rentz for always being in my corner. Thank you to Haley Crigger and Chase Atherton for reading earlier drafts of this novella and making it shine.

Finally, thank you to Hendrik. I love you more than words can say.